AFTER THE DOOR OPENED

By Gary Pisarski

Nightengale Press
A Nightengale Media LLC Company

AFTER THE DOOR OPENED

For information about Nightengale Press please
visit our website at www.nightengalepress.com.
Email: publisher@nightengalepress.biz
or send a letter to:
Nightengale Press
10936 N. Port Washington Road, Suite 206
Mequon, Wisconsin 53092
Library of Congress Cataloging-in-Publication Data

Pisarski, Gary
After the Door Opened/ Gary Pisarski
ISBN:1-933449-38-1
Family/Marriage

Copyright Registered: 2006
First Published by Nightengale Press in the USA

November 2006

10 9 8 7 6 5 4 3 2 1

Printed at
Lightning Source Inc.
1246 Heil Quaker Boulevard
La Vergne, Tennessee 37086

In memory of PC

The fun was always in that not told.

Chapter One

As the heels and soles of his shoes unavoidably tapped the tiles of the main aisle, Frank's eyes were fixed upon the polished casket lying ahead at the steps leading to the white marble altar. He shuffled sideways into the last vacant row of pews behind the small mass of heads bobbing up and down and turning side to side as the echoes of clearing throats, escaping coughs, soft voices and faint whispers bounced in the expanse beneath the high ceilings.

The muffled sounds were soon overcome by a more dominant set of tones reverberating through the air from an unseen organ. Moments later a priest adorned in a white robe emerged from a door on the side of the altar stage, taking his place in a tall backed chair of oak between two sitting boys, both half his size. By chance, though it now appeared older and the hair atop it grayer, the face of the pastor was one once familiar to Frank. He had last seen the man at another Chicago parish some forgotten number of years before.

The last note bellowed from the organ was the cue for the priest to begin his ceremonious routine. Frank's eyes followed his movements while his ears listened to the cleric's voice. When the mourners in the pews ahead of Frank rose to their feet, he also stood. When they sat down upon the wooden benches, he also sat. When they shuffled forward pushing their knees into the cushioned rests just above the floor, he remained sitting. And near the end of the service, when many of those before him proceeded to the base of the altar steps to receive the white wafer representing the body of Christ, Frank remained where he was, from where he observed the hands and facial expressions and the movement of the bodies returning to complete the imperfect circle back to their place in the long rows of waiting stalls.

In the procession to the cemetery, Frank drove alone at the rear of the line, turning off the radio as his thoughts pulled him into imaginary conversations with the man now enclosed inside the casket. He had not seen the man alive in seven years, looked at him briefly at the wake, and would never see him again from this day forward. Those mourning and those condoling reassembled around the open grave once again at the green cemetery, the blue of the spring sky dimmed by the dark lenses of the sunglasses Frank had slid into place over his nose and ears. The priest, now dressed in black, read aloud briefly from a book held open in his hands. He flushed the sunlight from the pages as he brought the covers together and announced the end of the service, signaling the range of faces that the time was appropriate to smile as they greeted one another with nods or extended hands or gentle hugs. A young boy in a little man's suit rushed from person to person, handing each a single sheet of paper that illustrated and explained the directions to the home of the daughter of the man laid to rest. And with the sounds of closing car doors and engines humming or rumbling to the turn of jingling keys, the glossy casket was lowered into the open grave by two men in time-worn brown overalls, their hands protected by heavy gloves.

Frank sat upon a plastic lawn chair alone at the back of the yard, placing his foot upon an emptied paper plate as a gentle breeze slid under one end, threatening to carry the stained white circle away. Out of the small crowd that had migrated to the patio at the back of the beige, aluminum-sided house, the priest headed towards Frank, his fingers curled around a brown glass bottle.

"Can I sit here?" he asked, pointing to the empty chair next to Frank.

"Help yourself," Frank glanced upward as he answered the man's question.

The priest sat, reached inside his coat for a cigarette, lighting it with a colored plastic lighter that he pulled from an outside pocket. He exhaled his first intake of smoke away from Frank. "So, why are you ignoring me, Frank?" he asked.

"I never like interrupting a man while he's working, Dave."

The priest lifted the bottle to his lips with his right hand, the lit cigarette held in the stubby fingers of his left.

"It's kind of early for that, isn't it?" Frank wondered aloud.

"I don't know. Is that why they have it sitting out here in tubs of ice? Besides, on my salary, I can't afford expensive brands like this."

Frank smiled at the man's reply.

"It's got to be what, ten or twelve years since I've seen you?" the priest guessed.

"Something like that."

"How did you know the deceased?" the priest queried.

"The *deceased*? Stan Burdette was my first partner when I made detective. We were together the three years before he retired."

"His daughter said he was somewhat hurt that no one from the department kept in contact with him."

Frank looked down for a moment under the weight of his own regret. "On his last day on the job, I told Stan that I'd call him...keep in contact. I called a couple of times in the first few weeks...even set a date to have dinner with him. But I had to cancel because of the job, and then I cancelled the makeup date. And I never called him again."

The priest was silent, nodding as his listened, alternating the bottle and cigarette to his lips.

"When Stan retired, he was a stocky, robust guy with a hearty laugh and strong handshake," Frank continued. "I didn't recognize the man lying in the casket at the wake the other night. The cancer did a number on him, Dave. He looked half the size I remember...and I never saw his hair as thin or as white as it had turned. I used to razz him when he colored his hair...teasing him for trying to look younger than his age."

The priest pointed the end of his beer bottle to Frank's hand. "I notice you aren't wearing your wedding ring. Did you and Mary split up?"

Frank looked down at his hand, stretching his fingers outward. "Yeah, she found someone who made more money than I did."

"Mary was a beautiful bride, Frank. And I've seen hundreds, if not thousands, through the years," the priest recalled.

"Well, beautiful women eventually marry money, Dave. You're lucky you don't have to worry about that."

"Is she remarried?"

"Yeah," Frank answered. "She married a defense attorney she met at work after the girls were old enough to go to school. They got their house for sale for $1.2 million because they want to move into something bigger. Me...I'm still living in a one bedroom apartment in a sixteen flat."

"I'm sorry the marriage didn't work out," the priest offered.

"Yeah, me too. When you married us, Dave, and told us it was for richer or poorer, Mary interpreted that as being she would stay married to me until she found someone richer."

"Well, there's always more to a break up between two people than something like that," the priest reasoned before returning the cigarette to his lips.

"The part you left out of the vows, Dave, was the part after until death do you part...the one that goes or until one of you wants out of the marriage."

"*That's* the state's way of making divorce easier," the priest said defensively. "The church tries to save marriage. You should have come to me for counseling."

"*Counseling* wouldn't have helped," Frank retorted, his inner bitterness roused by the very word.

Neither man spoke for a few seconds before the priest inquired, "How old are the girls now? What were their names again?"

"Molly and Megan," Frank answered.

"Right," the priest acknowledged, smiling at the answer. "How could I forget that? Mary, Molly, and Megan McKay. I liked the sound of that when I baptized the youngest girl. That was Megan, right?"

"Yes, she's eighteen now. Molly is four years older."

"*Really*!" the priest exclaimed, stunned at the measurement of time passed. "Do you have a good relationship with them?"

Frank shook his head from side to side. "They live out in one of the richer suburbs. Molly calls me every couple of weeks or so, but Megan...she adores her stepfather and thinks anyone in my profession is lower than the people he defends."

The priest nodded his head up and down suggesting that he understood, but Frank's words were but a fraction of the feelings simmering below his guarded surface. No human can read through the complexities of another in a few looks or words shared. Frank knew that. He had long ago abandoned hope that his thoughts would ever find refuge in another.

"I haven't seen your father since I was transferred out of the old parish. How is he?"

"I've got him in a nursing home on the North side."

"I pray for your mother's soul very often," the priest said softly. "I'm sure she's with God now, Frank."

"Yeah," Frank nodded his agreement. "Though I can't understand why she went before my father. He was always the mean SOB when he was drinking... and that seemed to be most of the time. The way he burned both ends of the candle, I thought for sure he would die before my mother did."

"And what about Mickey?"

"Mickey is turning out to be a copy of my father," Frank answered the query about his younger brother. "He can't hold down a job, and what money he does get in his hands, he either drinks or gambles away."

The priest shook his head, smiling. "Remember back in high school...when we both made the all city team playing ball for Lane Tech?"

"Yeah," Frank remembered.

"You had that nasty curve that no one could hit. And me...I thought I was the next Johnny Bench or Yogi Berra. We thought for sure we were going to end up in the majors together. Remember those times, Frank?"

"I do."

"Look at us now," the priest leaned forward. "A priest and a policeman."

"Well, look at it this way, Dave," Frank reassured the man next to him. "At our age we would have been washed up ball players by now. But we can still be a priest and a cop."

The priest smiled and thought about Frank's answer for a few moments before asking, "You like what you do, Frank?"

"It's a paycheck. And if I'm lucky, I'll get a pension when I retire and get a part time job somewhere to fill my time. What about you, Dave... have you been a good priest?"

"I haven't molested anyone if that's what you're asking me," the priest answered directly into Frank's dark blue eyes. "I've kept my hands to myself."

"That's not what I meant," replied Frank.

"Well, these days the public seems to wonder if we're all as weak as the few who get all the bad attention."

"Dave, as many times as I've seen things like that on the nightly news or read about them in the papers, I never thought of you as being one of those perverts."

"Thanks," the priest replied. "I was ordained with one of those men, Frank. Looking back, I still can't see signs of a man who would end up doing what he did."

"We seldom do, Dave. At least not beforehand."

A few seconds passed in silence before the priest could no longer hold back another question on his mind.

"I noticed in church that you weren't following along with the others," he said after a deep breath. "Don't you believe in God any longer?"

"Of course I still believe," Frank answered. He leaned towards the priest, resting his chin in the valley between two of his knuckles. "Me and God got this thing going where he knocks me down and I get up. Then he knocks me down again and I get up once more...and on and on and on it goes like that. I believe he gets his jollies every time he kicks me in my Irish fanny."

Frank shifted his body to the other arm of the chair before continuing. "Yeah, I know...he'll have the last laugh on me. But I figure if he's going to torture my soul, I might as well make him work for it."

The priest looked away, then back at Frank again. "You make it sound like God hates you,

Frank. He doesn't hate anyone. God guides some of his children through life on paved roads, well lit and dotted with plenty of food and refreshment. For others...he guides them through dense forests and scorching desert sands. But *either* way, he guides all his children home to the same place."

Frank looked into the serious eyes of the priest, giving out a short chuckle quickly topped with a wide smile. "How many times have you used *that* one?"

"It's what I do, Frank," the priest answered in a defensive tone dripping in frustration. "How did you get so bitter?"

"Experience," Frank answered, placing his hand on the priest's back. "I'm sorry, Dave. I guess I've been out in that scorching desert so long that some of my brain cells have been burnt off."

The priest took one final drag of smoke from his shortened cigarette, exhaled the cloud from the side of his mouth above and past a squinted eye, and then rubbed what little remained above the cigarette's filter across the sole of his black shoe. He flicked the tan butt into the thick bushes behind his chair. He held the brown bottle to the sunlight, looking at the small amount of liquid swishing back and forth on the bottom, and then tipped the neck towards his mouth and swallowed what remained.

"I guess I'll have myself one more beer and mingle from person to person offering my words of comfort," he said through a weak smile as he pushed himself up from the chair next to Frank. "Who knows, maybe I'll get lucky and one of these people will wake up tomorrow morning and remember something I say today."

"It was nice seeing you again, Dave."

The priest nodded in reply. “Frank, you know where to find me if you ever feel the need to talk.”

“Don’t keep your door unlocked,” Frank answered. The priest turned away, his eyes tilted towards the bending grass beneath his shoes as he withdrew in silence towards the house.

Frank again sat alone for a few long minutes in regret, his thoughts returning to Stan Burdette. He reached into his inside pocket, flipped open his cell phone and punched in a number on the little keys overmatched by the size of his fingers.

“Hey, this is Frank. Would it be okay if I stop by?... No, I’m not on the job today, I’m attending Stan Burdette’s funeral...Yeah, it’s as good as these things go. Is Angie at work?...You want me to stop on the way to get you anything?...I’ll be there in about an hour...Are you doing okay, Vince?...Okay, we’ll talk when I get there. See you in a bit.”

Chapter Two

It had been almost three months since the incident that threatened Frank's partnership with Vince Corelli and almost a month since the two had last seen one another. Vince and his wife Angie had gone through a difficult year, burying their only two children within a ten month span. Their older child, Franny, was only eleven when Vince and Angie heard that shocking word Leukemia, and for a year they struggled with the ups and downs in her health against the barrage of chemotherapy and medications.

After a period when the routine of blood drawings finally began to show a leveling of negative results, Angie believed that a day in the sun might lift her daughter's spirits, if not her's. She took Franny, the Corelli's son Carlo and a friend of Carlo's to Oak Street beach on Chicago's lakefront early in the previous summer.

While Carlo and his friend played in the cool waters of Lake Michigan, Angie sat contently with Franny on a blanket contoured over the miniature hills in the littered sand, treasuring each smile, each glimmer of life in Franny's radiant brown eyes. Then Carlo's friend appeared in the crowd of sunbathers, running towards Angie with his feet lifting the beach behind him. She was at first embarrassed by the angry faces looking his way, then irritated as his stop sent a spray of sand onto Franny's light skinned legs.

But as soon as the boy's tears and frantically spoken words cried that he could not find Carlo, the sudden fear blinded Franny's existence from her mother as Angie rushed into the fringe of the grayish-green water, calling and calling, then screaming Carlo's name.

The divers from the fire department found the boy's body three hours later, and the child that had not been the reason for their anguish, was gone. They had not yet begun to learn how to deal with Carlo's death when Franny's disease took her as well, leaving Vince and Angie childless, their hearts numbed by the devastating loss.

Then came the call, and Frank and Vince responded to the scene of a double homicide in a brown bricked bungalow on a city block lined with cookie-cutter houses, each one looking like every other. Inside however, the lifeless body of a 12-year old girl lied in an unnatural position on a blood soaked couch a few feet away from the soon-to-die figure of her 10-year old brother. The younger child was crouched forward over the control unit of a video game, the animated figures frozen on the red splattered screen of the television while the music of the game continued to loop from the speakers. Through a door-less opening connecting rooms, their mother sat at a table in the kitchen. Cereal boxes and bowls with milk at their bottoms were pushed to one side against plastic cups with an inch or less of orange juice remaining in each. A uniformed officer stood over her, his eyes guarding each movement as she lifted a dish towel to her nose and puffy, red eyes. Back in the room filled with death, another officer met Frank and Vince and shared what information he had gathered of the incident in the short time he was there.

The woman, distraught because her husband had moved out of the house, shot both of her children before sitting down at the kitchen table where she planned to take her own life next. But as she told the two uniformed officers, she could not bring herself to squeeze the trigger of the weapon one more time.

The officer's words enraged Vince, whose own two children taken from he and Angie would have been the same ages as the two children lying innocently in their own blood. He walked silently into the kitchen as Frank moved away to turn off the unwelcome sounds coming from the television. Vince drew his service revolver, jolting back the woman's head with her hair grasped in his hand. He recklessly pushed the barrel of his gun into her mouth, yelling at her, shouting obscenities, calling her names that no man should ever call a woman.

"You don't have the guts to do it?" he shouted down at her in anger. "I'll do it for you!"

After a long stretched-out moment, the officer next to the woman broke out of his momentary surprise and pushed Vince away with the weight of his own body. The barrel ripped at the inside of the terrified woman's mouth as the tightly gripped handgun followed Vince's retreating hand. Frank and the other uniformed officer rushed in from the next room to help restrain Vince. He struggled in vain against their overpowering strength before his body surrendered to the floor, his covered face soon sobbing as his torso and legs shook uncontrollably. The two paramedic teams who had entered the house as the police officers converged on the kitchen could no longer help the 10-year boy and soon turned their efforts to Vince. And there was no way of hiding what had happened.

With the children from the neighborhood in school and the working parents away, Frank easily found an open area along the long cement curb and parked his car in front of Vince and Angie's home. He placed his handgun in the glove compartment before stepping out to the street. The lawns of the houses on either side of the light brick home were well manicured, as green and tidy as the grass of Wrigley Field. In contrast, the lawn in front of Vince and Angie's home was long, dark, and strewn with outcrops of crab grass, both yellow and white dandelions, and rolled newspapers that had not found their way to the slightly elevated step at the foot of the front door. Frank extended his look down the long line of lawns on either side. All but Vince's flowed in conformity with the others. It was apparent to Frank that he had been the last person to run a mower over the Corelli's lawn, during the final week of Vince's hospitalization. It wasn't that the image of the grass mattered to Frank; but after Franny and Carlo, and the Chicago Cubs, Bears, and Bulls, the condition of the lawn was a favorite subject of Vince in his conversations with Frank over their countless hours together on the job. And they had been partners since shortly after Stan Burdette's retirement.

Vince opened the front door, his hair covered arms crossing his body with his hands tucked beneath his armpits. His faded white, sleeveless T-shirt, blue sweat pants, and bare feet were a stark contrast to the suit and tie and shiny black shoes worn by Frank.

"I was beginning to think you forgot about me," Vince said as he turned away, stepping towards a well positioned recliner facing the flickering screen of a large television. "I haven't seen you since I got home from the loony bin."

"I thought you and Angie needed the time to be alone," Frank responded.

"Why?"

"Because...you were away from each other for more than two months. Isn't that reason enough?"

"It doesn't matter. Nothing matters any more," Vince said softly, expressing his words by shaking his head of thinning hair.

Frank stepped towards the television, pushed a button turning the screen black, and sat down on a cluttered couch. Strewn across the carpeted floor were items of clothing, magazines, and sections of newspapers. The top of the scratch-worn coffee table in front of his knees was equally muddled with empty coffee cups, a beer can, and a half-consumed bag of pretzels. "Are you taking all your meds?"

"Are you my mother now?" Vince responded.

"No, I'm not your mother," Frank answered. "You just sound depressed. Damn it, you look awful, Vince."

Vince stared ahead at the screen of the television set, his reflection looking back at him.

"I'm taking all my medication," he surrendered. "It's just that it affects the manly functions of my body."

"There are pills for that," Frank offered.

"It wouldn't matter to Angie. She doesn't seem to care one way or the other," Vince claimed, looking down as he slid his hands back and forth over the material of his sweats. "I think she was having an affair when I was locked away with the other loonies."

"First of all, you aren't a nut case, Vince. You didn't belong in there. So do yourself a favor and stop calling it a loony bin and yourself a loony. If it wasn't for the politics, the department would have gotten you out of there long before now."

Vince glanced at Frank briefly before returning his eyes to the comfort zone of his own hands.

"Secondly, Angie wouldn't do that to you."

"How do you know?" Vince looked back to Frank sharply.

"I know," Frank answered. "C'mon, she's been through the ringer herself. She lost both of her children and then her husband had a breakdown. This isn't just about you, Vince. Angie needs the time to heal just as much as you do."

"You can't understand."

"Try me, Vince."

"It's just that...in the first few weeks I was in... *that* place, she was so sad. And then she got real happy, happier than I've seen her in years. And when I told her the doctors were releasing me, she got sad all over again."

"She was probably just worried," Frank said after a pause in his thoughts. "She's been on a roller-coaster of emotions over the past couple of years. She was probably happy that you were getting better and worried that you wouldn't stay on track when you got home."

"I'd kill him, you know," Vince said after a few seconds of silence.

"You'd kill *who*?"

"The guy she's had an affair with."

"You wouldn't kill anyone," Frank stated.

"I wanted to kill that woman...I really did, Frank," Vince answered back quickly. "I came so close. I think I would have done it if you and the other guys didn't pull me away from her."

"Well, you didn't."

"They'll never let me be a cop again," Vince sighed.

"They will," Frank said weakly. "Right now the DA's office is trying to protect their case against the woman. And *her* lawyer is trying to milk the police brutality angle to work out a deal giving her as little time as possible. When all that is worked out, you'll be back. You might not get back on the street right away, but you'll be back."

Vince tensed his body in the chair, moving his arms to his side, his hands resting beside him.

"Aren't you going to ask if I have any guns in the house?" Vince asked.

"Okay. Do you have any guns in the house?"

"No," Vince answered. "The department took my service piece and Angie hid my Glock."

"I thought you also had a Beretta?"

"That's up in Milwaukee at my parents place," Vince answered. "But that doesn't count. It's not in this house."

Frank pushed his body up slowly, walked over to a set of book shelves, and grasped a picture frame containing a snapshot of Franny and Carlo with Angie.

"That was taken a few weeks before Carlo drowned," Vince said from the safe haven of his chair. "It was still in the camera when he died. We didn't get the film developed until a few months after he was gone."

Frank gazed down at the picture as the three smiled back at him. His finger slid over the glass following the arch of Angie's long, black hair from where it rested on one of her shoulders to her other. Franny's head tilted towards her mother, resting against the side of Angie's upper arm. On the other side of Angie, Carlo faced forward with an abundant smile, his thick eyebrows pushing his forehead up into a head of hair as curly and dark as that of his mother.

"I named the kids after my parents," Vince's voice again sounded from over Frank's shoulder. "Francesca and Carlo. It was my way of preserving the memory of my parents when the day came for them to pass. Instead, my mother and father had to see their namesakes get buried first."

Frank gently placed the picture frame back on the shelf. "I'm sorry, Vince," he said, turning to face his friend.

"I know, everyone tells me they're sorry. But that doesn't bring my kids back."

"No, I don't mean just about Franny and Carlo," Frank explained, "I'm sorry I didn't foresee what would happen when we saw those two kids lying in that house. I'm sorry I didn't act fast enough to stop what happened. I'm sorry there were others in the house and I'm sorry that we couldn't keep what happened just between us."

"How do *you* do it?" Vince asked.

"How do I do what?" Frank asked, unclear of the meaning of Vince's question.

"In all of our years together, you were always the one on the edge, always the one ready to lose it. But you never did."

Frank shrugged his shoulders. "I don't know. A lot of times it was all for show. And when it wasn't, you were my safety valve. I don't know, Vince."

The two men were silent as the seconds passed, each listening to his private thoughts during the pause between the spoken words.

"Who is your new partner?" Vince asked.

"Lula Briggs."

"Briggs?"

"Yeah."

"She's a good cop," Vince reasoned, "She's always had a thing for you, you know. Too bad she's black."

"She's my partner," Frank replied quickly. "Her being black has nothing to do with it."

"Black or not, partner or not, you still need to find yourself a woman," Vince asserted.

Frank looked at his watch, uncomfortable that the conversation had taken a turn with *his* life as the potential subject. And though Vince suddenly seemed more at ease to not talk about himself, Frank was not about to cross that line. This time belonged to Vince.

"Thanks for coming over, Frank," Vince said, recognizing the fidgeting and indirect looks of his friend. "And if I never told you before, I could never have survived the loony bin if it wasn't for you and Angie visiting me as often as you did. Thanks fo being there."

"Yeah," Frank acknowledged.

"Angie wanted to have a get together in the back yard for family and friends...you know...for my benefit," Vince confessed quietly. "But I told her to forget it. I feel more comfortable around you than anyone else I know. Either way, you know where I am if you've got the time to stop by again."

"That's the second time I've heard that today," Frank said before leaving. Seeing Vince again was more difficult than he thought it would be. It didn't take much effort on his part, and perhaps had he followed through on his easy promises and visited or called Stan Burdette when he could have done so, he wouldn't have felt so much regret over the death of his first partner. But sitting in his car, looking back up the walkway to the closed door of Vince's house, the guilt of the last few months felt no lighter after this visit.

Chapter Three

Lula Briggs was a beautiful woman, almost too beautiful to be a police officer—something she heard numerous times throughout her years on the force. But beauty was never a blessing to her while growing up on the mean streets of Chicago's South Side—nor did beauty provide an education or a way out of her violent, dirty, and hope-starved neighborhood. The Army provided that escape. And after four years, her time in the service eventually led her to the police academy where she met her first husband, who three years and one child after their wedding was gunned down on the same streets where Lula roamed as a child and young girl. And she vowed that her son Jamal would never have to walk those same streets.

Lula's smooth brown skin glowed beneath the brilliance of her dark almond-shaped eyes. The upper boundary of her top lip curved attractively from a gentle, middle dip, up and then down again to the corners of her mouth. Like most every mother with a college bound son, she carried a few more pounds than admitted on her driver's license. But the smartly shaped dark gray jacket and black silky blouse beneath camouflaged any slight imperfection that only she would recognize anyway.

She was leaning against the wall at the top of the precinct steps when Frank arrived in the morning after the day of Stan Burdette's funeral. "Good morning, handsome," she called out to him, a bright smile warming her face as she held up a small, white sheet of paper. "I hope you're ready to roll because the boss gave us one to start off the day."

"Great, just what I need after a bowl of oatmeal," Frank replied. "Where's this one at?"

"Just relax and follow me," Lula said as her smile lingered from one word to the next. Frank's eyes followed the details of her movement down the steps. "It's my day to drive, so you can sit in the passenger seat and tell me all about your day off."

"What about the SOCO team?" Frank queried as he inhaled the sweet scent of lightly applied perfume drifting in her wake.

"They're probably there already," Lula answered, referring to the scene-of-crime officers.

There was no need for Lula to check the address scribbled on the small paper rectangle she had been given by her Lieutenant. The two white and blue squad cars and the coroner's van parked in front of the five story building made it clear they were at their destination. A uniformed officer at the front door directed them to the third floor, where they met another emblem attired officer standing outside an open door to an apartment in the middle of a short hallway. A detective, in protective clothing, was too focused on brushing powder around the edges of the door to acknowledge Frank and Lula. And if he did, his voice would have been filtered through the light blue mask shielding his nose and mouth. His wedding band pushed its presence from beneath the thin covering of the department issued latex glove on his busier hand.

"What do we have here?" Frank asked the blue shirted officer in the hallway, a man whose youth was advertised in the smooth complexion of his face and the dark color of his short cropped hair.

"The building manager called early this morning after the tenants on both sides of this apartment complained about a burning smell in the hallway. We found a dead guy inside and a pot on the stove containing over-cooked food."

"Who is he?" Lula asked.

"Damon Grayson...age fifty-five...this address on his driver's license."

"What was that name again?" Lula asked.

"Damon Grayson."

"Do you know him, Lu?" Frank asked.

"No."

"Does he live here alone?" Frank asked the officer, writing down the information within the horizontal lines on a page in a small navy-blue covered notebook.

"According to the building manager, a young girl lived here also. But he hasn't seen that much of her over the past few weeks."

"Where is this building manager?" Lula asked.

"In his apartment," the young officer answered, "Number 1B. I told him not to go anywhere until he heard from us."

"I'll go down and talk to him, and then begin interviewing the neighbors," Lula said, tilting her head up to Frank. "You want to manage the scene?"

"Yeah, that sounds good."

"The tenants on either side of this apartment are at work now. They were gone before we had a chance to ask them any questions," the young officer looked at Lula, his voice apologetic in tone.

"That's okay, we'll get to them later," Lula assured him before walking away. She had been in his shoes before. She knew the feeling of being new to the job, wearing a uniform, and being the first on the scene only to hand off the information to senior officers. And she herself had known detectives who remembered what it was like to wear a uniform, and she had dealt with detectives who had forgotten.

"Getting any good prints, John?" Frank asked the blue masked man, still in his crouch as he swirled powder around the door knob.

"Plenty here, Frank. I'll let you know."

Frank stepped through the doorway into the crime scene. The victim's body had fallen to the floor between a love seat and coffee table, both of which were smeared with red lines of blood pointing towards his body. His left leg had moved last, resting over the right leg just under the knee. A richly red splotch stretched from under the collar of his white shirt down to his mid-section and down his left side and onto the light gray carpet beneath him. The victim's eyes stared blindly at the underneath surface of the coffee table top. Frank's eyes quickly turned away from the man's open gaze.

"He took two to the chest and there is no trace of a weapon, so I doubt this gets ruled as a suicide," a voice rang out from an adjoining room.

"Hey, Bali," Frank greeted as he turned to face the technician from the coroner's office, a tall thin figure whose diction gave no indication that his family moved from India when he was eight years old.

"It looks like a small caliber. I'll let you know after we get him on the table and dig out the slugs."

"How long do you think he's been dead?"

"Well, it looks like he was cooking himself dinner when he was killed, so I'm guessing twelve hours or so. How is that for a scientific answer?"

"Who else is here?"

"Sal Martin and Ted Schwack are working the victim's bedroom," replied Bali, pointing to a hallway.

Frank looked around the room of the murder, sneaking another quick glance at the body. He had seen more than enough bodies over the years and was content on letting the pictures satisfy any questions unanswered by the coroner's reports or the evidence gathered by the SOCOs. The room looked neat and tidy with the exception of the area around a big-screen television, where DVDs and video tapes and empty plastic and paper-board sleeves were scattered on the floor, with a few remaining on a set of shelves where they had all been stacked side by side at one time.

The apartment had two bedrooms. Frank passed by the first, looking in through the doorway without stepping into the room, carefully not placing his hands on the wood trim around the open door. The walls of the room were light lavender. The carpet was a lesser white than that glossing off the two dressers or the headboard of the queen-size bed. The mattress was covered by a patterned comforter, pinkish in theme. It was a room decorated with a feminine touch.

Flashes of light darted from the doorway of the other bedroom as a tall man with a retreating line of black hair clicked his camera.

"Hey Schwack," Frank called out as he entered the second bedroom, "I overheard my boss saying you were the photographer for his son's wedding. I didn't know you could take pictures of breathing people."

"Very funny, McKay," the photographer sparred back from above his camera.

"This clearly was no robbery, Frank," the other man in the room spoke up. "This guy had three hundred bucks sitting on the top of his dresser and a couple of grand inside his sock drawer."

"Did you find any forced entry, Sal?"

"No, none. This guy let the shooter in, and whatever happened after the door opened is the knowledge of only two people, one of whom is dead."

"Anything else, Sal?"

"Yes," replied the short, thin man in a pale blue shirt and red tie, the crown of his head void of any visible hair from Frank's position in the room. "I found two checks written to him for a grand each, dated a month apart."

Sal stepped over to a chair where he had placed his evidence case, a slight limp reminding Frank that the officer leading the evidence team had been wounded in the line of duty years before. He lifted a plastic bag containing two checks and walked over to Frank, his shoes covered by blue booties.

"I'll fax over copies of these after I get back to the office, but you may want to jot down the name on these checks...Doctor Kale Epson."

"Thanks, Sal, that's a start. Lu and I will have a talk with the good doctor. These are dated on the 1st of the last two months, so maybe they're nothing more than rent checks."

Sal smiled upward to Frank, "Well, that's what you're here for. It's your case."

"Did you guys see that mess of DVDs and tapes in the other room?"

"I took pictures, McKay," the photographer said from the opposite corner of the room. "And Coomer is going to dust them for prints when he is done with the door."

"I'd like to make a list of what is there, just in case I can find a way of determining what movies are missing."

"We'll take care of that, Frank," Sal assured him.

Frank looked over Sal's shoulder to a desk on which a computer monitor sat cockeyed, the screen shattered.

"What do you make of that?" he asked.

"Don't know, yet," Sal answered. "If it was the shooter, he didn't know much about computers. He demolished the monitor, but didn't touch the CPU."

"What about that blinking light?" Frank continued to probe. He pointed to a blue light on the front of a tower unit nestled in a rectangle cubicle at the bottom right of the desk.

"I see your aversion to computers hasn't changed, Frank," Sal chuckled in response. "The CPU is in sleeping mode. It was either on when the shooter came in, or he turned it on when he got here. John is going to dust the keyboard, monitor, and main unit before we're done."

"Are you taking all of that back to the lab?"

"Yes, we'll check out his computer activity and files and give you a heads up if we find anything," returned Sal.

"Hey, McKay," the photographer called out. "Do you want any wallets of the vic's body or just eight by tens?"

"My wallet is busting out with your work as it is, Schwack. Just give me the larger prints."

"We'll be done here in a couple of hours, Frank," Sal added.

"Did you do that bedroom across the hall?"

"No," Sal answered, "We'll get to that after we process the kitchen and finish the room in front after Bali removes the body."

"I'm going to do that right now if Ted has all his pictures," Bali's voice blurted out from the doorway.

"I've got what I need," the photographer announced.

"Okay, I'll try to have a prelim to you guys by late today or early tomorrow," Bali said as he turned to leave.

"Leave me a message when you have the caliber," Frank shouted to the open doorway before turning back to face the two men in the bedroom. "Can I check out the kitchen?"

"Sure," Sal answered as he reached into his evidence bag. "Just don't touch anything. And put on these booties and hair cap."

"You guys aren't wearing hair caps," Frank protested.

The photographer looked up from his camera again. "That's right, McKay. But unlike you, what hair we have left is hanging on for dear life."

Frank pulled the blue coverings over his shoes and dye enhanced brown hair, and squeezed each of his hands into a pair of latex gloves taken from his pocket. He stood at the doorway leading into the kitchen for a few moments, his eyes moving slowly from left to right, from object to object, his mind imagining what human activity took place in this room the night before. Moving forward, his distorted reflection on the side of a chrome pot met him as he stepped closer to the stove. The inside bottom of the pot was charred black in the center, surrounded by a brown crust, the burnt odor still seeping, if now faintly, over the rim.

Three of four chairs around the white-legged kitchen table were tucked beneath a green vinyl covering. In full view away from the table, the fourth chair was angled slightly, perhaps done so when the victim pushed away before standing to answer the door. A clean knife and fork rested upon an equally gleaming dinner sized plate next to a half-filled cup of stagnant coffee set off to the upper right from the open chair. Atop the table, an open check book with the victim's name and address, a pen, a roll of stamps and sheet of return address labels, and two envelopes. One of the envelopes, the address of the electric company showing through a rectangle opening in the otherwise white paper, stood upright, resting against a salt shaker, the return address label and stamp in place.

The second envelope, almost square in shape, was eerily incomplete, the victim's return address in the left hand corner, a stamp in the right. Missing were the three lines identifying the addressee's name and address. Frank reached into the side of his suit jacket and pulled out a small pocket knife. With the open blade he bent down and gently lifted the flatly sitting envelope, noting it was sealed. He scanned the table again, and the counter tops around him, and crouched down, his eyes skimming the tiled floor and the seats of the chairs beneath the table.

"Have either of you guys seen an address book?" he inquired after walking back to the bedroom where Sal and Ted continued to work.

"Not yet," replied Sal.

"Me either," added Schwack.

"Keep your eyes open for one while you're processing the rest of the place," Frank commanded. "Sal, there's a greeting card in a sealed envelope on the table in the kitchen. I need to see that card as soon as you finish with it."

The photographer pointed his camera at Frank and with a click the room was jolted with another flash of light.

"What was that for, Schwack?" Frank demanded, realizing the camera had been pointed towards him.

"You look cute in that blue cap, McKay," the photographer answered with a smirk across his lips.

Frank pulled the cap from his hair and dropped it on the bed. "I'm going to check on Lu," he said, turning towards the doorway.

Sal Martin followed Frank into the hallway, "Hold up a second, Frank."

Frank stopped, looking forward at the activity of John Coomer and Bali, who had placed the victim in a black vinyl bag, and the bag onto a wheeled cart. Sal moved ahead of Frank, looking up at him. "I'm sorry to hear about Stan Burdette."

"Yeah, me too."

"Did you hear about Vega?"

"Luis Vega?"

"Yes. They paroled him two weeks ago. He's back in Chicago."

Frank opened his hands and gestured with his arms apart. "So?"

"I just thought you should know, that's all," Sal replied. "Just watch your back."

"I will. Thanks."

Frank found Lula in the hallway outside the apartment. "You find out anything, Lu?"

"Yes," she responded. "The building manager had a name, address, and phone number for the dead guy's son. He lives near Wrigley Field, but his wife said he's at work now. She gave me an address where we can reach him...it's in the Loop. I also found out that our victim was accosted outside the apartment building last week."

"Was there an arrest?"

"Sounds like it," Lula replied. "The manager didn't see what happened. It was one of the tenants who called it in. Supposedly a squad car responded and a couple of our guys took the perp away. I'll check for a police report when we get back to the house."

"Well, let's first track down the son and inform him that his father is dead."

Chapter Four

Frank didn't like the part of the homicide investigation involving notification of the next of kin. It was never easy and seldom as anticipated. He was never comfortable going into the homes or the workplaces of strangers, knowing he first had to interrupt the rhythm of someone's day or night with news that often devastated or forever altered their lives. And then, he had to wait for the initial shock to subside and the sobbing to peak before he could probe the survivors with questions. Stan Burdette had a knack for these situations; he could read people's eyes and sense the rise and ebb of their emotions. Stan knew the proper words and when to speak them to vanquish the walls that make people strangers to one another. Frank never succeeded in emulating his first partner's gift.

In his seven years with Vince Corelli, the two men alternated the two components of the notification task. On one case, the detective who did not break the bad news was the man who pressed for answers. On the next case, they switched roles. It worked well that way for Vince and Frank, so they never changed. During interrogations however, when it was needed to play the game, Frank was more effective and at ease being the bad cop, leaving Vince to perfect the role of good cop. But then again, Vince was a good cop. They were good cops together, earning a reputation as one of the more successful pairings in the precinct.

Lula brought to their partnership her own preference in the notification roles, one with which she was comfortable. And in her opinion, her way carried a higher degree of sensitivity for the survivors of the deceased. She insisted on being the partner who broke the bad news and asked follow up questions to all African-Americans and all women. She relinquished the role for all others to Frank.

The victim's son, Trent Grayson, worked in one of the granite clad buildings in the heart of Chicago's downtown area, on one of the streets named after a president. Frank knew all them by their street names. He could never answer the order that the presidents served their nation, but he knew the order that they appeared in Chicago's Loop: Washington, Madison, Monroe, Adams, Jackson, Van Buren, Eisenhower, Harrison, Polk, Taylor, and Roosevelt.

The sandy-haired man in white shirt and yellow tie exited the elevator and headed directly to the reception desk in the lobby, turning just as Frank and Lula approached him from behind. The security guard at the lobby desk had called him a mere ten minutes earlier, barely time enough for Frank and Lula to get comfortable in the black chairs along the lobby wall.

"What's this about?" he asked. "Are my wife and children okay?"

"This has nothing to do with your wife and family, Mister Grayson," Frank answered. "Is there somewhere we can talk with some privacy?"

"You can use that conference room," the guard interjected, pointing to a door on the side of the lobby.

The victim's son led Frank and Lula into the narrow room in which a long table was bordered by three plush chairs on either side. Frank and Lula sat on one side opposite from where Trent Grayson cautiously, anxiously placed himself, his hands on the table, clutched together. He looked nervous, alternating his eyes between Frank and Lula as he awaited their voices.

Frank leaned forward on his elbows rested upon the table with his finger tips from one hand matched up with those from the other forming an open triangle. "Mister Grayson, there's no easy way to say this. Your father was found dead in his apartment this morning."

"My father? What was it, suicide?"

"No, he was murdered," Frank answered.

"Murdered? Who killed him?"

"We don't know yet. I'm sorry."

The victim's son pushed away from the table, his back held against the support of the chair, his hands grasping the ends of the armrests. He showed no outward emotion. He did not cry, nor did he appear to be under pressure to restrain his tears.

"Do you have the right man? Damon Grayson?"

"According to his driver's license picture, I'm sorry that we do."

"You need me to identify the body?"

"Yes, we'll need you to do that."

"When?"

"I'll have the coroner's office call you, or you can call them if you'd like."

"Why did you ask if it was a suicide?" Lula queried.

"Wishful thinking, I guess."

"What does that mean?" Frank asked.

"Nothing," the man answered, nodding his head as he brought his hands together in his lap. "My father and I were not very close. He divorced my mother about twelve years ago, and she never got over it. She committed suicide and...I guess since then I've wished that my father would come to know the suffering and despair that drove my mother to take her own life." Trent Grayson's words were like the aroma seeping from hot apple pie just out of the oven. Frank could taste them in his own mouth, though his own parents never divorced and he never broke away from his father.

"Where were you last night, Mister Grayson?" Lula asked.

"What?" he replied, surprised by the question. "Um, my son had a little league game. My wife and I took the kids out for ice cream afterwards."

"Do you own a handgun?" Frank inquired.

"No, never. We have three kids in the house. I wouldn't think of owning a gun."

"Do you know if your father had an address book?" Frank asked.

"I don't know. Ask Jennifer."

"Who is Jennifer?" Lula requested.

"She's one of the reasons I could never patch things up with my father."

"And you tried to do so?" Lula pressed on.

"I tried. I wanted my kids to have a grandfather. My wife's parents live in Florida and we only see them once a year."

"Why didn't it work out?" Lula asked.

"Jennifer...she was the reason," he answered, running his hand over his forehead and through his hair. "It was a weird situation. She had to be sixteen years old at the most when she moved in with my father. It just wasn't right. My oldest daughter was eleven at the time."

"How did he meet her?" Frank asked, looking up from his notebook for a moment.

"I don't know. She just showed up. And my father and Leo made her the center of their lives."

"Who is this Leo person?" Lula asked.

"Leo Salerno...my father's business partner."

"What kind of business?" Lula responded.

"I've never been quite sure."

Lula looked up from her notes. "The manager from your father's building told me that a young girl lived with your father, but he hadn't seen her for awhile. Do you know if Jennifer was still living with him?"

"I don't know," Trent Grayson replied, "Check with Leo. I suspect that she bounced back and forth between my father's place and his."

"Do you have his address?" Frank asked.

"No."

"How long ago was this when you thought she was sixteen?" Lula questioned.

"Four to five years."

"Do you know her last name?" Lula continued.

"I don't know her real name, but Goodman is what she used for the movies."

"She's an actress?" Lula asked.

"If you call showing up on screen for a few brief seconds. My father sent me two DVDs of movies in which he landed her bit parts. In one she just screams when a bad guy takes her purse. In the other she's a waitress with a two-line exchange with the main character."

"What were the titles of these movies?" inquired Frank, his pen in hand waiting to jot those down in his notebook.

"I don't remember," Grayson's son answered with a shrug of his shoulders. "They were both filmed here in the city. I can call you later or email the titles to you after I get home."

Frank and Lula both slid their business cards across the table in the man's direction. "Contact either one of us when you have that information or can think of anything else that might help," Lula said. "And again, we are very sorry for your loss."

Trent Grayson gathered both cards in his hand, stacking one in front of the other. "I only wish my father would have paid as much attention to his own grandchildren as he did to Jennifer."

Chapter Five

"McKay, you've got yourself a visitor," the desk sergeant peered over his glasses as Frank and Lula entered through the front door of the precinct house.

Frank turned in the direction indicated by the end of the pencil in the officer's hand. The young woman handsomely dressed in a black skirt and peach blouse had already set to motion her approach towards Frank, her auburn hair pulled over and behind her left ear. Her face was alive with a bright smile wide beneath sparkling eyes of a hue floating between those of olives and emeralds.

"Molly," Frank called out. "What are you doing here?"

"Is there anything wrong with me wanting to see my Dad?"

"No, of course not. I'm just a bit surprised."

"And who is this, Frank?" Lula asked as she stepped alongside the father and daughter. Only Frank was mindful of the attention aroused in the room full of police officers and the assortment of transient characters that would rather be elsewhere.

"Lu, this is my daughter Molly," Frank answered, an easy smile slipping across his lips. "Molly, this is my partner—Lula Briggs."

The two women exchanged greetings, with Lula boasting about the good qualities of the man they stood near, exaggerating on the frequency at which Frank talked about Molly and her sister. She then excused herself, “I’m going upstairs to make some calls, Frank. I’ll see you in a little bit.”

“She seems nice,” Molly said as Lula ascended the stairs. “What happened to Vince?”

“He’s on vacation,” Frank lied.

Molly looked up at her father, barely able to contain the excitement beneath her smile. “I need to tell you something, Dad. Can we go somewhere else for a moment?”

“Sure, let’s go outside.”

Once outside, and away from the eyes in the precinct house, Frank hugged his daughter tightly. “It’s so good to see you, Honey. I miss you so much.”

“I know, Dad,” Molly responded, her right hand covering the top of her left hand as they stepped apart.

“So what do you want to tell me?” Frank asked.

Molly extended the fingers of her left hand, their raspberry tips followed by the sparks of light dancing from the diamond set upon a bright silver band. “I’m getting married, Dad.”

Frank gently slid his hand beneath his daughter’s, her soft skin resting effortlessly upon his.

“It’s beautiful, Honey. And the lucky guy is?”

“Blake, Dad,” Molly answered. “You met him a few months ago at Christmas.”

“I remember him. Isn’t he still in college?”

“He’s got one more year of law school, Dad,” Molly answered, placing her hand on the side of her father's arm before continuing. "I know you aren't thrilled about lawyers, considering that Mom married one, but Blake really is a good guy. And we are very much in love."

"Hey, as long as he doesn't have a criminal record and he treats you well, it doesn't matter to me what he does for a living."

"Thanks, Dad. What you think is important to me."

"When is the big day?"

"The first weekend in December."

"A winter wedding?"

"Yes."

"Well," Frank responded, "Why not!"

The smile eased off Molly's lips. "Dad, there's one more thing I need to tell you about the wedding."

"What?"

"Mom and Rick are paying for it."

Frank looked at her for as long as he could before his discomfort forced him to turn away. Molly's words were a reminder that for several years he had been on the outside of his daughters' lives, separated by miles and time. What was real in his life was what he had missed by not seeing his daughters every day, not kissing them good-night each evening, not answering the door when their dates arrived, not hearing them laugh, or cry. All of that was a daily reminder blurred in the echoes of the emptiness in his life.

"And they are also giving us a down payment on a house," Molly added. She was sensitive to her father's place well enough to fear that he would take the financial news of the wedding as a personal slight. She was also aware that he didn't have the kind of money that could pay for a wedding or match the generous gift offered by her mother and step-father. "I don't want you to worry about the money or feel bad that Rick is paying for it. I still want you to be the one who walks me down the aisle to give me away."

Molly's innocent choice of words ignited a response in Frank's thoughts that he held back in silence. He never wanted to *give up* Molly or her sister Megan. He never wanted to lose them or their mother. But by the time his wife had fallen in love with Rick, there was nothing that Frank could say or do that had the power to keep them all together. "How can you give away something you don't have?" he thought to himself.

"What does your mother think about me walking you down the aisle instead of Rick?"

"It doesn't matter what she thinks, Dad. My wedding is *my* day and you are *my* father."

"What about Megan?" Frank asked. "Do you think she could stand being in the same room with me?"

"Megan is a spoiled brat, Dad," Molly answered with a roll of her eyes. "But I can guarantee if she had the chance to dance with you, she would delight in being your little girl again."

The sound of the words 'little girl' put pressure on Frank's eyes, forcing him to take in a deep breath through his nose.

"You'd be surprised how amazingly the two of you are alike," Molly added. "Just like you, Megan is a softie under a tough outer crust."

Frank gazed at his daughter's face, taking in the happiness radiating from her eyes. He pulled her close, resting his chin on the top of her head. "Congratulations, Sweetheart," his words whispered tenderly. "I'm very happy for you."

Frank's cluttered-top desk was butted up against the neatly arranged desk of Vince, the latter left as it was the last time Frank's previous partner had sat there. Lula rose from the chair at her desk and stepped across the aisle just as Frank settled into his. "You never told me that your daughter was that pretty," she said.

"Yeah," Frank replied. "Did you get anything on the Grayson case yet?"

"Yes. I've got an address for Leo Salerno and one for Oliver Jackson."

"Who is Jackson?"

"He's the guy who was roughing up our victim last week. Thing is, Grayson refused to press any charges and Jackson was released."

"Did you talk to the arresting officers?"

"One of them...he said Jackson was mouthing off and they had to threaten him with adding on a resisting arrest charge to calm him down. But Grayson insisted on not pressing any charges, saying it was a personal matter."

"Does this Jackson fellow have a record?"

"A couple of traffic tickets...that's about it."

"Who do you want to see first?" Frank asked.

"Salerno is nearest," Lula answered. "But the Lieutenant wants us to stick around so he can talk to us."

"Great," Frank responded in a low mutter. "There's nothing I like more than a trip to the principal's office."

Lula straightened her posture, placing her slender hands upon her hips. "Frank, you've got to get over your resentment at him. He's just doing what is best for the department."

"That's a bunch of BS, Lu," Frank responded, trying to muzzle the anger in his voice. "He should have had the guts to stand up for those of us who work for him. Vince deserved better than being sacrificed to make things easier for the DA. Tillman should have had Vince's back...not stabbed him in it."

Lula knew when to back off. "I have a home phone for Jackson," she said, giving her an excuse to go back to her desk. "I'll call to find out if he's there or not."

The man who was first out of the Lieutenant's office was well-dressed, his custom tailored suit looking out of place as he made his way through the maze of aisles between the desks and file cabinets of the squad room. Frank recognized the man's grim, clean face, but could not immediately recall where he had seen it before, or the name that belonged to it. Lieutenant Tillman followed a few steps behind, looking professional in honey-brown slacks, indigo shirt, and a muted red tie. He looked distinguished in his gray and white hair, each strand perfectly sprayed in place.

"McKay and Briggs," he called out, "My office."

Frank and Lula followed the commanding figure through the open doorway past the frosted glass door that bore his name in black lettering: "Lieutenant Barry Tillman". He closed the door behind them as they each sat in one of the chairs a few feet in front of his polished wood desk, a privilege of his rank, notably larger than the gray metal desks to which the detectives outside his office laid claim.

"Do either of you know who that was?" he questioned as he took his place in the high-backed, black leather chair on his side of the barrier. Both Frank and Lula shook their heads indicating they did not.

"Wade Donovan," he answered their silent replies.

"The Mayor's brother?" Frank questioned.

"Yes, one and the same. And do either of you know why he was in here?"

Again, neither Frank nor Lula could answer the Lieutenant's question.

The Lieutenant slammed his open hand on the top of his desk, "Because he wanted to tell me how to do my frickin' job, that's why! It turns out that this Damon Grayson who was killed last night is a business associate of the Donovan's and they're worried this will somehow torpedo the Mayor's run for the Governorship."

"Wait a minute...how did *he* find out so quickly?" Frank asked.

"You know, McKay," the Lieutenant said pointing his finger at Frank. "That is exactly what crossed my mind while I was sitting here with my thumb up my butt, unable to answer any of the questions he had about the case."

"Well, he didn't here it from me or Lu...and I doubt he heard it from the SOCO guys," Frank declared. "My guess is that he was told by Grayson's son after we notified him of his father's death."

"Or maybe it was Grayson's building manager," Lula offered.

"Lieutenant," Frank leaned forward. "It wasn't one of us."

The Lieutenant eased back in his chair, his piercing eyes upon Frank and Lula. "What do you have so far on this?"

"Definitely a murder...two shots to the chest," Frank began. "No forced entry. It probably went down last night between six and nine. We have two possible leads plus one missing girl and a business partner we need to interview."

"We'll have more when Sal Martin and the coroner's office give us their findings," Lula added.

"Wasn't this a robbery?" asked the Lieutenant.

Frank shook his head. "Not at first glance. The victim had a stash of money in plain view."

"Are you sure?"

"Yeah. Why?" inquired Frank.

"Because Donovan specifically mentioned more than once that I should let him know what was missing from the victim's apartment," the Lieutenant answered. "He offered to pull strings with the robbery division to get me whatever help I needed."

"Lieutenant, if we do find out that anything is missing, we *may* want the guys in robbery to keep their eyes open," Lula voiced her opinion.

"I want both of you to listen to me," commanded the Lieutenant, holding his finger less than an inch over his thumb. "I am this close to making Captain and I don't want to get screwed over this case. If it gets solved, I want it solved under my watch. If it gets too hot to handle, we'll get rid of it. The Mayor will be watching this one. Can I make things any clearer?"

"No...I get the picture," answered Frank.

"So do I, Lieutenant," Lula replied.

"Good, now both of you get out of here and get on those leads," the Lieutenant ordered. "And keep me apprised."

"Okay, we'll keep you *apprised*," Frank said sarcastically as he stood and turned towards the door.

"Don't mock me, McKay," the Lieutenant said sharply. "You're not talking to one of your street thugs."

Frank followed Lula through the opened office door without turning back to answer the Lieutenant.

Chapter Six

The address for Leo Salerno took Frank and Lula to the northern edge of Chicago's Gold Coast on Inner Lake Shore Drive. The building overlooked the blur of passing cars, buses, and trucks, beyond to the blue-gray expanse of Lake Michigan. White sails crawled in the background and white rectangles moved more quickly closer in, leaving splashes of their color behind upon the water's surface. The air was fresher, the sidewalks cleaner, and the leaves of the trees greener than those in the neighborhood in which Frank lived. Or so it seemed.

It was obvious to both detectives that the young woman who answered the door wore nothing more than her skin beneath the clinging lime shirt not long enough to meet the top of her matching shorts. The curls and waves in her strawberry blonde hair had yet to be tamed for the day, the faint freckles on her upper cheeks were not yet hidden by powder, and the red on her misty lips had softened overnight.

"We're from the police department," Frank announced as he and Lula displayed their laminated identification cards. The young woman's electric blue eyes circled past the faces in the small pictures upward to those of the two detectives, settling to meet Frank's gaze. Frank could not help but shift his stare back and forth to both of her eyes, the gripping color of which was amplified between perfect circles of black set against a white background. “Is Leo Salerno here?”

“Leo!” she screamed out, turning her head away. “There’s someone at the door to see you.” The shrill of her voice shook off the temporary attraction that drew Frank to her eyes.

A short, middle-aged man came into view behind her, his eyes looming large behind the thick lenses of his glasses. “Who is it, Jennifer?” he asked as he neared the doorway, his slightly overweight figure filling out his round frame.

“Jennifer?” Frank noted, “Jennifer Goodman?”

“Yes,” she answered tentatively, the energy in her curls fading in a fraction of a moment after catching up with the swing of her head.

“Good,” Frank replied. “We need to talk to both of you. Can we come in?”

They followed Salerno into a room with a large window with a mesmeric view of the lake. Salerno soothed his body into an oversized, deep chair as the two detectives sat down on a plush, ivory couch, the lighter color contrasting with the skin of Lula’s hand as she skimmed her palm over the velvety material. Jennifer stood to Salerno’s right, both of them staring at Lula’s milk chocolate skin. Lula’s dark eyes mirrored the light filtering through the large window as she returned an uncomfortable smile in their direction.

Frank began with a question. “We understand that Damon Grayson is your business partner?”

“More so in the past than in recent history,” Salerno answered slowly, choosing his words with care.

"What does that mean?" Lula probed further, the sound of her own voice easing the awkwardness slowly creeping over her senses.

Salerno glanced at her for a moment before turning to Frank to answer. "Let's just say that we reached a point where the directions in which we both chose to move was...shall I say...no longer the same."

"When did the both of you last see Mister Grayson?" Lula asked, no longer able to maintain the imposed smile forced upon her lips.

"Three weeks ago," Salerno answered with a flip of his chin in Lula's direction.

"And you, Jennifer?" Frank asked.

"The same."

"We understand that you lived with Mister Grayson," Frank continued. "Is that correct?"

"What is this about?" Salerno interrupted as he lifted his arm, fanning the fingers of his hand in front of Jennifer's face.

"Mister Salerno, please let Miss Goodman answer the question," asserted Frank, softening his look towards Jennifer after a sharp glance at Salerno. "I saw your bedroom in his apartment. Did you live there?"

Jennifer looked down at Salerno briefly until she received a signal that she could answer. "Yes, I moved out three weeks ago."

"And what was the reason?" Frank asked.

Jennifer hesitated while she searched for the words, "I just didn't want to live there any longer. That's all."

"Is that the last time either of you talked to him?" inquired Frank.

"What is the reason for all of these questions?" Salerno insisted. "What is going on here?"

Frank and Lula exchanged glances before Frank turned back to face Salerno and Jennifer. "Mister Grayson was murdered last night."

Jennifer's hands rose to cover her face, muffling the slow groan of her oncoming tears through a low voice repeating "Oh no...oh no," as she turned away. Salerno twisted his body around the back of the chair, observing her as she scurried out of view, the sound of her weeping trailing behind like drifting smoke. He slowly recoiled back to his forward position, his head shaking off the disbelief of the detectives' news. "Who killed him?"

With a subtle nod of his head, Frank motioned Lula to go after Jennifer before he acknowledged Salerno's question. "We don't know at this time. We talked to his son, who told us you were Grayson's business partner. We came here looking to get some insight into the man's life, hoping it might provide us a lead or two."

"Am I a suspect?"

"Mister Salerno, to be honest with you, anyone we talk to is considered a person of interest. No, that doesn't mean that I'm sitting here, viewing you as a suspect at this time. It doesn't mean that you need a lawyer. You can make this relatively quick and painless, or you can make it as difficult as you want. If you feel uncomfortable answering my questions and you want us to leave your home, just say the word. I can always have you brought in for questioning by a couple of uniformed officers."

Salerno stared back at Frank with his magnified eyes. "Okay. I've seen enough movies to know you will want to ask where I was last night. I was here alone after seven. That's when Jennifer left to go out for awhile, visiting a friend. I was sleeping when she got home. I heard her, but didn't look at the clock. If you need my DNA, blood, hair or anything else, you can have it. You will find my fingerprints and other traces of me at Damon's apartment because I spent a great deal of time there. And the answer to your ultimate question is no, I did not kill Damon."

"Do you own a handgun?" Frank asked.

"No," he answered.

"Do you have any idea who might want to see Mister Grayson dead?"

"Damon wasn't the most honest man I have known in my life," answered Salerno, his eyes looking away before his thoughts spurned him to plead back to Frank. "I need to get into his apartment. There are things in there that are sensitive to our business dealings. I need to find out if anything is missing." He stood, clearly having turned nervous, rubbing his hand over his tinted black hair.

"You can't do that, Mister Salerno," stated Frank. "The apartment is a crime scene and everything in it is now considered evidence."

"Can I get a court order or something?"

"No," Frank answered. "Nothing appeared to be missing, Mister Salerno. There was a couple of thousand dollars in cash left untouched. His wallet and watch were there. The only disturbance seemed to be that either someone was searching through his collection of movies, or they were knocked over in a struggle."

"What about his computer?"

"It wasn't taken," Frank answered. "It might

help if we could have Jennifer walk through the place. She might notice if anything is not where it should be."

Salerno did not answer. He continued to pace the room, rubbing his face and running his hand over his hair as he continued to fret, showing more emotion outwardly at the thoughts running through his mind than he did at the news of Grayson's death.

"Do you know Oliver Jackson?" Frank asked.

"What?" Salerno answered, his worry interrupted by the detective's question. "No, I never heard that name before."

"What about Doctor Kale Epson?"

"He might be Damon's doctor," Salerno responded. "I heard the name, but never met the man."

"And Wade Donovan?"

Salerno stopped the nervous shuffling of his feet. "Yes, Wade is the one who arranged for Jennifer to get parts in movies being made in the city. That's the source of our parting with Damon."

"Why exactly?"

Salerno returned to his chair. "Damon and I had put Jennifer through acting classes and singing lessons—the whole package. At first we leaned on Donovan to get her a part, our way I guess of trying to remain heroes in her life. To our surprise, she has a real presence on screen, and her last director felt she had raw talent. Jennifer and I wanted to move her in that direction, but Damon balked...he wanted to put a stop to it."

"Why?"

Salerno hesitated, deciding to place a cap on

the amount of honesty he would share. "I don't know why."

Lula followed Jennifer into a back bedroom, sitting gently on the bed next to the young woman whose body had calmed as her sobbing softened with the remains of her tears. Lula laid her hand soothingly on Jennifer's back.

"When I learned that my husband had been killed, I reacted much the way you did," Lula spoke softly.

"I didn't mean for him to die," Jennifer looked up, the whites of her eyes red with sadness. "I didn't mean it."

"You didn't mean what?"

"The last time that I saw Damon, I told him that I wished he was dead and out of my life," she whimpered in a shaky voice. "They were just words. I didn't mean them."

"I know," Lula responded. "We often say things we don't mean to say, and they always hurt the most when we cannot say we're sorry."

Lula leaned over, trying to make eye contact with Jennifer. "Jennifer...I need to ask you something. Was Damon your lover?"

"No."

"Is Leo your lover?"

"No."

"Jennifer, I need to know where you were last night."

"I was out with a friend."

"I need to know the friend's name so that I can verify what you are telling me."

"I can't tell you that."

"Why? Was it a man?"

Jennifer did not reply.

"Jennifer, was it a man?"

"I can't tell you that," the young woman answered. "I don't want Leo to know."

Lula looked at the doorway, extending her neck to increase her view into the other rooms. "Jennifer, were you with Wade Donovan?"

Jennifer looked up at Lula with her eyes wide, eyebrows raised, and her mouth open. "How did you know? You can't tell Leo. Please, I beg of you, don't tell Leo."

"I won't," Lula answered quietly. "But don't tell anyone else."

Chapter Seven

Oliver Jackson's address could not be any more different than that where Leo Salerno resided. With Lula driving, Frank absorbed the details of the streets on the other side of the glass from the advantage of the passenger seat. In his silence he was struck by the contrast in vehicles. Whereas the newer, shiny car or SUV was commonplace along the Gold Coast, they were rare on the dirty streets bearing numbers rather than names. The older models had migrated to this neighborhood south of Chicago's Loop, their outer shells rusted and dented, their windows marred with zigzagging lines, and many with their wheel covers missing. Frank thought that his own car would appear out of place in either of these areas of the city.

The tired skin, gray-haired woman at Jackson's address identified herself as his mother. She didn't hesitate to tell the sweet speaking Lula that her son could be found at a tavern located on a nearby street corner. Frank stood smartly in quietness in the dusk-drawn shadows, a few steps down from the old woman's sight on the creaking, weather-worn wooden stairs.

The neon lights glowed through the iron bars covering the glass on the two windows on either side of the tavern's heavy entrance, the tired hinges moaning as Lula pulled the door towards her. Frank's eyes scanned the dark corners through the haze inside, his search halting at two middle-aged men standing over a pool table with a prominent slice of gray duct tape clinging to its exhausted green surface. His eyes moved again to the bar, where two more men sat, separated by three empty stools, both peering over their shoulders at the well-dressed detectives. Frank's skin tone alone was enough to identify him as a police officer to the eyes cast his way. High in the corner behind a tall black man standing behind the bar, the sound from a television roared for a moment as a batter ran to 1st base, the leftfielder bending down to retrieve a white dot that appeared to be one of many floating diagonally across the screen.

"There's a white man in the house," one of the men proclaimed in a deep voice. "Hold onto your billfolds."

"Which one of you is Oliver Jackson?" Frank responded loudly.

"It depends who's asking," the talkative man at the bar replied.

Frank identified himself and Lula as police detectives, pulling back his jacket to reveal the shield hooked upon his belt. In the dim of the lights however, none of the patrons bothered to look at it.

"The name is Ollie Jackson," the man who had spoken first declared, turning his head back to take a sip from a tall glass half-filled with beer. His dark eyes looked into the mirror behind the bartender, watching the reflection of the two intruders as they moved towards him.

"We're here to ask you about your beef with Damon Grayson," Frank said, pushing aside the empty stool to Jackson's left while Lula flanked the man on his right.

"I thought he dropped the charges against me," defended Jackson. "You tellin' me he changed his mind?"

"He was murdered last night, pal," Frank answered. "And we heard you argued with the man last week, so we want to find out why."

"You ain't stickin' this on me!" Jackson replied excitedly. "I know how you police operate. Some white piece of trash gets killed and you want to put the blame on a black man."

"We're not blaming anyone," Frank disputed.

"Clyde," Jackson turned to the bartender. "You tell them where I was last night."

"The same place you is every night," the bartender replied. "With your big black ass on your favorite stool."

"I saw him here," one of the men at the pool table blurted out.

"Me, too!" kicked in the other.

"Ollie, it sounds like you've got an alibi for last night," Lula said from his right. "But we still want to know why you went after him."

"The man stole money from me."

Frank sat down on the stool, placing his elbows on the cushion covering the edge of the bar. "How did he steal money from you, Mister Jackson?"

"Like you're going to believe me!" Jackson protested. "I've tried to tell all kinds of white people what that man did to me, and there ain't one who was willing to accept that a white man can steal from a black man. They all say the same damn thing. It was my fault, like I'm the dumb black man who ain't smart enough to know anything."

"We want to know," Lula said, placing her hand on the top of his shoulder.

"*You* want to know?"

"Yes," she replied.

"And what are you going to do about it? If the man is dead like you say he is, he ain't gonna pay back what he stole from me."

"Please," Lula requested.

Jackson took another sip of beer and returned the glass carefully upon the wet circle from where it was lifted. "When things were going good and I had a job and a family, I hit five numbers in the lottery. You know what that was to me? Almost three grand after the government grabbed their share. Three grand...I never had so much money in my life."

"What did you do with it?" Frank asked.

"Oh, I had plenty of ideas for that money, but my wife told me to invest it. I told her that only rich white folks invest money, but she told me that her friends where she worked did it, and lots of them wasn't white."

"Did you invest it?" asked Lula.

"Not right away, I didn't."

"Did you put it in the bank?" Lula inquired.

Jackson laughed. "Who do you think I am... that Ronald Trump guy? I ain't never had enough extra money to stick in no white man's bank. I ain't like you rich police. My wife come home from work one day and told me to call Grayson. She got his name from some friends of her's."

Jackson finished what beer was left in his glass and asked the bartender for a refill before he continued talking. "Grayson talked me into investing what was left of the three grand into some new stock for some new company. My nerves were a wreck at first, but my wife started bringing home a newspaper from work and we followed that stock every day. A few months later my three grand was worth double. I felt like I was livin' the white man's dream."

"So you made money," Frank stated.

Jackson took another sip of beer and looked at the detectives' reflections in the mirror behind the bar. "My wife was so excited that our lottery money was growing that she upped and went to night school at Malcolm X College to learn about stocks. Then Grayson started calling me two, three times a day, telling me our stock was soon going to be worth garbage. He wanted me to sell before it was worth nothing."

"And you held onto it?" Frank asked.

"No, I sold it just like he wanted me to," answered Jackson. "My wife told me not to sell, but I told her I was the man of the house and I would make the decision. So I did what Grayson suggested and bought a new stock for the six grand that I sold the first stock."

Jackson paused to lift the glass to his lips again. "He told me that's how I'd get rich. But then my wife showed me the newspaper six weeks later. That stock he talked me into selling for six grand was worth forty grand. You hear what I'm saying? If I had listened to my wife I would have had forty grand. That white son-of-a-bitch lied to me. And when I called him back, they told me he no longer worked for them."

"But you still made three grand…right?" Frank asked.

"No, the second stock was worth nothing after the whole country went bad. Then I got laid off from my job and my wife kicked me out of our flat. And now I live with my mother and spend every night sitting here lookin' at Clyde's ugly face. My whole life's gone down the toilet 'cause of that white man."

"Playing the stock market is like playing the horses, Jackson," Frank shook his head. "You should have known there's never a sure thing."

"That's what I mean," Jackson exclaimed in a sigh of frustration. "It all comes back to you white folks telling me it's all my fault."

"What was the name of the firm where Grayson worked?" Lula asked.

"You mean when he ripped me off?"

"Yes," she answered.

Jackson turned to Frank. "Can I reach in my back pocket without you shooting me?"

"Yeah, I'll control myself," Frank countered.

Jackson pulled out his old wallet, the worn leather bearing as many lines as the palms of his hands. His fingers lifted out a beaten business card, which he handed to Lula.

She smiled as her eyes moved over the black raised letters. "Crosswhite Investments...you know the meaning of irony, Ollie?"

Jackson ignored Lula's comment, turning to the bartender instead. "Give me a shooter of your house whiskey, Clyde." He looked forward at the mirror behind the bar, his stare at Frank's image. "I ain't getting my money back, so I guess the next best thing is to drink to the man who killed that white crook."

Chapter Eight

The invisible flow of heat barely had time to cool Frank's morning cup of coffee when Sal Martin slid onto the chair next to the detective's desk, his head reflecting the fluorescent rays dropping from the ceiling.

"Good Morning, Pretty Lady," Sal smiled over to Lula. She responded with a silent wave, the receiving end of her phone pressed against her ear. The father of two was a rarity who dared to call a female coworker "pretty lady" and got away with the compliments that often followed. But the women police officers who knew Sal sensed the innocence of his intentions. Perhaps it was the brotherly aura in his friendly smile. But they knew, and as Lula did, they enjoyed the safety in his wordplay.

"I checked the fax machine this morning, Sal," Frank greeted the slim, balding man. "I thought you were going to send me a couple of things on the Grayson case."

"I thought I'd drop them off in person," answered Sal as he settled in the "guest" chair. He lifted the lid of the black attaché case lying flat upon his lap and created a clearing on the surface of Frank's disordered desktop by moving things to one side. "I'm going to lay some papers on your desk, Frank...but I'm not responsible if you can't find them in this chaos." He began extracting sheets of paper and laying them in the clear space he had created. "Here's the list of DVDs and movies that were in the apartment. Here's a copy of the two checks from Doctor Epson. We're holding on to the originals. Coomer lifted a good number of prints from throughout the apartment... but of those he has looked at so far, none match the second set of prints on the checks."

"So you don't think the doctor was in the apartment?"

"No, no, no," Sal answered. "I'm just saying that he didn't touch anything. Coomer also found a kaleidoscope of body fluids and hairs on the bedding in both bedrooms. It's lucky for us that your victim didn't change his sheets very often."

"Did you get any matches to any of it yet?"

"Not by name, Frank," Sal answered. "But we did find matching hairs in both rooms—some male, some female."

"That's interesting. We interviewed the girl who had lived with our victim and she told Lu that she and Grayson weren't lovers."

"Is that girl named Jennifer?" Sal inquired, his hand returning to his briefcase.

"Yeah, how'd you know?"

Sal lifted a plastic bag containing an opened greeting card. "This was in that envelope on the kitchen table," he said as he laid the bag in front of Frank. "The only prints on the envelope were those of the vic."

"Do you miss it, Sal?"

"What?"

"Doing what I do."

"Sometimes," Sal shrugged his shoulders. "Then again, I like what I'm doing now."

Frank slanted his head downward, his eyes moving over the handwriting inside the card.

"By what the vic wrote there, I'd say he had pretty strong feelings for this Jennifer," surmised Sal.

"Yeah," Frank replied. "If you saw this girl, Sal... you'd swear she was Grayson's daughter or grand-daughter."

"What do you have there?" Lula asked, resting one hand on Sal's shoulder.

Frank lifted the plastic bag to her waiting hand. "It looks like our victim wanted Jennifer to come back home. He wrote the words please and promise enough times."

"Do you think this Jennifer is the shooter?" Sal asked.

"No," answered Lula without lifting her eyes off the greeting card. "She was out last night. I already called the girlfriend she was with to verify her story."

"Did you get anything off the computer, Sal?" inquired Frank.

"Nothing unusual," Sal responded. "It was all rather boring, and no files that contained names or addresses."

"And still no address book?" Frank asked.

"No. But I do have the results of the autopsy," Sal remembered. "I told Bali that I was coming over, so he gave me your copy. He found two thirty-eight caliber slugs in your victim's chest. One punctured the outer wall of the heart."

"I guess that was enough to kill him. When will John have the results on the unidentified prints and stuff from the bed?"

"These things take time, Frank. He sent it over to the lab. You'll know as soon as we know."

Frank looked up as the door to the Lieutenant's office opened. The distinguished looking, neatly coiffed man summoned Frank and Lula with the hook of a finger. He closed his door behind the two detectives and moved to his desk. He stood erect in an intimidating stance, lifting a stapled set of papers from the neatly arranged surface.

"I read your preliminary report, McKay. Haven't you ever heard of a dictionary? You've got more spelling errors in here than I would expect from a ten year old."

"It was late, Lieutenant. I didn't know I would be graded on grammar," Frank sneered.

"You're slipping, Frank," the Lieutenant replied as he dropped the papers back to his desktop. "You were probably the best cop I had in the squad before Corelli lost his marbles. I don't know what the hell is going on with you, but I need you to get your crap together for this case."

Frank bristled inside at the Lieutenant's comment about Vince, but held his thoughts behind his clamped teeth and tightened lips.

The Lieutenant pressed on with his scolding. "I'd be embarrassed to show this report to the DA or to my bosses…or to any 4th grade teacher. If you can't handle writing reports any longer, then give it to Briggs." His eyes challenged Frank to respond, and when he felt he had made his point, he asked, "Now, where the hell are the two of you on this case?"

"We've ruled out two of three suspects," Lula spoke up, covering for the fury beneath Frank's silence. "This may have been a love triangle, but we are fairly certain that robbery was not a motive."

"Do you have more suspects in line?"

"We are heading over to interview another person of interest after we leave here," Lula answered.

"Then get out there. You aren't doing me any good standing around my office." The Lieutenant dismissed the two detectives with a gesture of his hand, fixing his eyes on Frank's face in anticipation of an exiting comment. But Frank continued to keep control of his words...for now.

Chapter Nine

Frank's anger at the Lieutenant simmered beneath his brooding exterior as he trailed Lula down the three wide steps leading to the street level outside the precinct's front door. It was there that Internal Affairs officer Peter Richter met them on the sidewalk as he walked in the direction of the aged building.

"Can I talk to you for a few minutes, McKay?" he asked, his hands tucked away in the pockets of his trousers.

"About what?" Frank replied with impatience dripping on the two words.

"Corelli."

Lula picked up the signal that Richter's request was not intended for her ears. "I'll get the car, Frank. But it's your turn to drive today."

As in any police force, there were men and women in the ranks who were cautious around their fellow officers from Internal Affairs. Richter and Frank however, were acquainted by a common history that dated back to their time together in the police academy, from where they graduated with only two names between them. That was the first of two intersections in their careers before Richter was assigned to investigate the Corelli incident. The familiarity of the two men had brought a sense of relief to Frank and in turn he made every effort to be accommodating with the intent that his cooperation would help his partner.

Richter led Frank away from the busy precinct entrance. “Frank, I just wanted to give you a heads up,” he began, looking around to avoid any of the others entering and leaving the building. “It’s not looking good for Corelli.”

“Don’t tell me that!” Frank said disgustedly.

“I’m sorry, Frank. Internal Affairs recommended counseling and reinstatement pending a release by medical, but the DA’s office is pushing for termination without pension.”

“That’s all political, Pete,” Frank protested.

“I agree. Vince has been a great cop. His record up to now has been flawless, but Mrs. Rellik’s attorney is pushing heavy on the police brutality issue.”

“That stinks. She killed her kids. Whatever Vince did doesn’t make her any less of a murderer.”

“I know what you’re saying. I don’t like it either. But the Mayor has his eyes on the job in Springfield and the DA is feeding the media frenzy with his own talk about zero tolerance on police brutality. I would also like to hear half as much about how terrible it was that the woman shot her own kids to death, but these muckity-mucks up the ladder have put all the focus on the department.”

“So what do I tell Vince?” Frank asked.

“Tell him to get a good lawyer.”

“That’s a crock of garbage, Pete. Vince deserves better than that.”

Frank started to turn away, but Richter’s voice stopped him. “Frank, I need to ask you one more thing.”

"What? Is the department coming after me next?"

"No...this is about Briggs."

"What about her?" Frank barked.

Richter held up his hand, signaling Frank to listen. "Briggs drives a new caddy and sends her kid to private school. How does she do that on a cop's salary?"

"I can't believe this," Frank reacted in disbelief. "Now you're going after Lu?"

Richter motioned to Frank to lower his voice. "It's just something that got noticed. You're her partner. I thought you might know."

"Look," Frank said, folding his arms with his fists clenched, "her first husband was a cop killed on the job, and she got a big insurance settlement. What's gone wrong with this department, Pete? They no longer support the good cops risking their necks on the street 'cause they're all too busy covering their own butts."

"Forget I asked," Richter responded.

"What's your angle with all this, Pete? Are you fishing for information on Lu in exchange for a favor that will help Vince?"

"No, the two have nothing to do with one another. I'm just doing my job, Frank.

Lula drove up in a gray car, honking the horn before sliding over to the passenger seat.

Frank moved his head forward, his chin near Richter's shoulder. He whispered into the man's ear. "You tell whoever sent you to get their nose out of Lu's life."

Chapter Ten

As he steered the unmarked car through the thick city traffic towards the hospital where they were told they could find Doctor Epson, Frank didn't tell Lula of Pete Richter's interest in her. He only told her about Richter's comments about Vince. It was true that Lula lived in a nice home on a quiet, clean street in an integrated neighborhood. And absent from Frank's recall was any memory of her complaining about a mortgage or the ever increasing Chicago real estate taxes, two subjects grumbled aloud by many of the other detectives. It was a running source of ribbing inside the house that she bought herself a new Cadillac every other year, and was seldom seen wearing the same clothes twice within any two week period. Perhaps the only boasting out of Lula's mouth however, was when she talked about sending her son Jamal to the top private school in the city. But Frank dismissed the reaction of the other cops in the squad as envy. And then again, everything that could be said about Lula could as easily be said about Lieutenant Tillman.

Frank didn't know Lula when her first husband was killed in a shootout with gang-bangers. It wasn't until after she ended her second marriage to an abusive drunk that she transferred into Frank's precinct. Frank never met him, but often wondered what kind of man would have picked the wrong woman to abuse.

Over the time he came to know her as a member of the squad, the thought teased Frank's mind a few times or more that had they met at some other point in their lives, they may have been more than what they were to one another. He felt an attraction, a connection to Lu, though he never quite understood what created the spark. Nor did he ever risk the effort to be rejected. He enjoyed joking around and talking and listening to her. He was drawn and took pleasure in watching her, whether she moved around in the squad room or just sat at her desk. When he and Vince were out on the street and returned to the precinct, Frank often searched for Lula's face as he entered the squad room. If she was there when he returned, his spirits were lifted. If her chair was empty, he felt disappointed—until she returned from the field. And he also found himself daydreaming of her on his time away from the job. But that was all before the incident that sent Vince to the hospital.

Now, Frank and Lula were at a different kind of hospital. They found Doctor Epson where they were told he would be, on duty in the emergency room of the small facility. Two uniformed officers stood outside the windows of the ER, watching through the glass as a physician stood over a man lying on a cart. The doctor's green surgical pants were partially covered by a white lab coat, a stethoscope hanging from his right pocket. Two nurses stood nearby, in colorful scrubs, their two pairs of hands in rhythm with the hands, lip movement, and glances from the doctor. The bottom of the patient's nervously twitching shoes were all that could be seen by the four police officers.

One of the uniformed officers held a white towel over his forehead, a red blotch of blood visible on the material held under his brown-skinned hand.

"What happened to you?" Frank asked, the badge on his belt in plain sight of the officers.

"That guy on the table smacked me with a wine bottle," he answered. "The doctor kicked us out of his ER."

"What happened to the guy on the table?" Lula inquired as she placed her hand gently on the officer's head and peeked at the source of the blood.

"We hit him back," the other officer answered.

"So why did the doctor kick you out?" Frank demanded.

"He said the perp needed attention before my partner did," the unhurt officer answered.

"Do you guys know where we can find a Doctor Epson?" asked Frank.

"That's him," the bleeding officer pointed with his finger pressed against the glass.

Frank's nostrils flared and his lips tightened as the anger heated the blood beneath his face.

"Frank!" Lula pleaded, reading his next move as he burst around her, pushing open the door leading into the emergency room.

"Who are *you*?" the doctor reacted to the sudden presence of the two detectives.

"Detectives McKay and Briggs," answered Frank as his eyes scanned the name on the front of the lab coat.

"I don't care who you are," the doctor scolded. "Get out of here. Wait outside with those other two cops."

"Pardon me?" Frank retaliated.

"Frank!" Lula pulled at his jacket sleeve.

"I told you to get out of here," the doctor ordered. "Do it now!"

"I'm not leaving until you tell me why you're working on this piece of garbage while an injured officer stands out there holding back his own blood?" Frank demanded.

"This man's injuries are worst than that cop out there. It's my decision. Now get out of here. I won't say it again."

"Like I said, *Mister* Epson," Frank argued. "I'm not going anywhere until I get answers from you. Then again, maybe you don't care if I arrest you for obstruction in an investigation. What about it, *Mister* Epson?"

"Frank," Lula pleaded. "We can wait until he's done."

"Listen to the lady cop and get out," the doctor snarled.

"Not until you tell me why you are paying Damon Grayson a thousand dollars each month, *Mister* Epson," Frank insisted, holding up the copies of the checks taken from the victim's apartment.

The doctor glanced at the paper held up in front of his face, stunned into a momentary loss for words. "It's a personal matter."

"Not any more, *Mister* Epson. This is a murder investigation. Your pal Grayson was killed the other night."

The doctor felt the eyes of his two nurses looking at him as the temperature in the room seemed to increase suddenly.

"I don't know anything about that," he stumbled through his reply.

"Are you sure of that, *Mister* Epson?" Frank continued to press him.

"For God's sake, will you stop that!" erupted the doctor. "Please call me Doctor Epson."

"Oh?" Frank said sarcastically. "Well, let me tell you something about that." He pointed towards the two officers on the other side of the window. "You see those two men. They are *Officer* Washington and *Officer* Jones. Do you see those uniforms? Those men risk their lives every day to protect tight asses like you, and they have earned...no...they *deserve* the respect to be called Officers. Do you understand what I'm saying *Mister* Epson?"

The doctor, nurses, and Lula were embarrassed into speechlessness, neither willing to attempt a response to Frank's controlled tirade. The wide-eyed man on the table however, forced a slight smile as he listened from his reclining advantage, his still feet no longer nervous.

"*I* can call them cops," Frank continued. "They can call each other cops. But *you*, you don't have the right to call them cops."

"Fine," the doctor surrendered quietly.

"Now, *Doctor* Epson," Frank went on, "Why don't you tell me about these checks?"

"Not in here."

"Then please lead the way," Frank said in a starkly changed tone, turning to the two nurses with a smile on his face before he followed the doctor through the doorway. "Will one of you be kind enough to take a look at that injured officer?"

Frank and Lula followed the doctor to an unoccupied room down the hall. The doctor closed the door behind him, motioning the detectives away from the entrance towards the room's window.

"Grayson was blackmailing me...a thousand dollars a month for the past four years."

"Why?" Lula asked.

The doctor was clearly upset. "You have to understand, Officers. If I tell you why he was blackmailing me, you'll arrest me. My career, my marriage, my whole life is at stake here."

"Are you into drugs?" Frank probed.

"No," he answered, rubbing his hands together as he continued to worry. "You have to understand...I have three children and I am a very good father...this is very difficult to talk about."

"Okay, let's take another approach to this, Doctor," Frank pushed forward. "Look at me. Look right into my eyes and tell me the truth. Did you kill Grayson?"

"Of course I didn't kill him!"

"And where were you two nights ago?"

"I was at home with my family. You can call my wife and ask her. Please."

"Okay," Frank responded as the doctor offered his cell phone. "If you didn't kill Grayson and your wife confirms your alibi, the worst possibility in my mind has just gone poof. My partner and I only care about finding Grayson's killer. We don't care what you did to get blackmailed. The man is dead. You don't have to pay him any longer. As long as you are being up front with us, that's good news number one."

"What is the other good news?" the Doctor asked.

"We all make mistakes. I can see it in your eyes that the truth is a heavy weight on your shoulders. My partner and I are authorized to give you immunity, but only if you come clean with us...now."

"How can you give me immunity?"

"As long as you haven't killed anyone, we won't hold you responsible for whatever it was that Grayson was using to blackmail you."

"My partner is right," Lula answered. "We have the power to grant in the field immunity."

"I've never heard of such a thing," the doctor responded.

"It's one of those powers granted under the Homeland Security Act," Frank answered. "We wouldn't lie to you. We are under oath to always tell the truth."

The doctor looked at both detectives, both of whom were using their experience to mask their performances with honest faces.

"Some years back...my wife and I were going through a shaky period. Grayson sold me some stocks. That's how I met him. He invited me over to his apartment one night and I had a few too many drinks. There was a young girl there as well, and I somehow ended up in bed with her. I went back there occasionally after that. I knew it was wrong. I mean it was wrong to cheat on my wife...but that girl made me feel good at a time when I needed to feel good. Then one day, Grayson showed me a video tape of me and this girl in bed. She had told me she was twenty years old, but it turns out she was much younger."

"Was her name Jennifer?" Lula asked.

"Yes," the doctor nodded. "Grayson told me if I didn't pay him a thousand dollars each month...he would send copies of the tape to my wife and to the hospital administrators. I had no choice. My whole career was at stake. I could have been charged with rape."

"Did you ever think of calling his bluff or threaten you would go to the police?" Frank asked in a softened tone offering solidarity to the man he had driven into this corner of truth.

"He wasn't bluffing. He gave me the name of another man he was blackmailing, one who *did* decide to stop paying."

"Did you contact this other man?" Lula asked.

"Yes. And I didn't want my life destroyed like it did his. Grayson went to the man's house when he wasn't home. He showed a video tape to the man's wife. I couldn't bear to have that happen to my wife, my kids—to me."

"Do you have a name and know where we can reach this other man?" Frank inquired.

"Harold Klinger. But his name won't do you any good unless you want to visit his grave," the doctor replied. "He committed suicide almost two years ago."

The doctor's hands were trembling faintly, and the air exhaled from his lungs sounded as if it had passed over a bumpy surface. He covered his mouth with one hand as he looked out the window, away from the detectives.

Frank looked at Lula as he placed his hand on the man's shoulder. "It's over, Doc. If your wife confirms your alibi for the other night, we'll just tell her it's about a patient and you won't hear from us again."

"But what is next?" he asked. "What will happen to me when you look at the video tapes? Will I be arrested? Will they be used in court? Will my wife see them?"

"We haven't found the tapes, yet," Frank replied, unable to answer the doctor's questions. "All I can tell you for now…is try not to worry about it."

Chapter Eleven

The drive from the hospital to the downtown office of Crosswhite Investments took only fifteen minutes in light traffic, but Frank and Lula sat in the lobby for another half an hour waiting to talk to the branch manager. Frank had stepped out for a few moments and returned, plopping down next to Lula, his head leaning back against the barely beige wall.

"I called Sal Martin and told him what we found out from the good doctor. I was thinking they may have missed something on Grayson's computer and in his apartment. But Sal says they did a thorough search."

"Nothing?" Lula asked.

"No," Frank answered. "What do you think about this guy Grayson, Lu?"

"I think he's starting to look like a real sleaze bag. No wonder someone shot him."

"What does your gut tell you so far?"

Lula looked over into Frank's dark blue eyes, his head turned towards her as he slumped back into a relaxing posture. "I don't like Leo Salerno. Maybe it's the way his eyes are magnified by his thick glasses. Maybe it's the way he avoided looking at mine because he was too engrossed gawking at the color of my skin. That man made me feel uncomfortable."

"What about Jennifer?" Frank asked. "How old do you think she is?"

"Twenty."

"Really? Jeez, guessing ages is something I just can't do any longer."

"Well, her driver's license claims she is twenty-two," Lula replied. "But I think she's only twenty."

"Why do you say that?"

"Trust me, Frank. I'm a woman. I know."

Frank surveyed the room before turning back to Lula again. "I'm not so sure Salerno is our shooter, but the relationship between him and Jennifer and Grayson is looking weirder by the minute."

The phone beeped at the receptionist's desk and she looked over to the detectives. "Mister Abbott will see you now. Just go right in."

The detectives forgot about the time they were left waiting to see the young man in his late twenties as he apologized and exchanged greetings with them with a cheerful delivery of his words. He covered his crisp white shirt and light gray tie with a suit coat before sitting back in his chair behind a desk smaller than that in Lieutenant Tillman's office.

"So what is this about?"

"Well, Mister Abbott...," Frank began before being quickly interrupted by the young man.

"Please, Detective," he insisted. "Call me Paul. With all due respect to both of you, please. Just call me Paul."

"Okay, Paul," Frank responded slowly. "We are here about Damon Grayson."

"Speak of the devil," Abbott returned quickly. "And I mean that literally. Think of the words shady, sneaky, and two-faced, and you have a good description of Damon."

"You didn't care for the man?" questioned Lula.

"No, and whatever you are accusing him of doing, I wouldn't doubt it is true."

"Well, Paul," Frank said. "We are here investigating his murder."

"Whoa!" Abbott sat back with open eyes. "So this is a heavy duty investigation. Whoa."

Frank exchanged smiles with Lula before answering the young man's response. "I've never heard it called that, but I guess you can say this is as heavy duty as it gets."

"Whoa!" Abbott exclaimed once again. Although neither detective had flinched from the chairs in which they sat, he motioned them to wait. "Don't go anywhere. I might have something that will help you."

He punched a button on his phone and spoke over the keypad without picking up the receiver, his voice filled with excitement. "Esther, please forward all my calls to whichever brokers are available. I am tied up in an important meeting."

"Whoa, this is exciting," he said as he turned his attention to Frank and Lula. "What do you need to know?"

Both detectives were surprised by the man's reaction, reminding Frank of the players on his baseball teams who sat on the bench for most of the game until the coach motioned them to take the field in the late innings. "Let's start by you telling us why you didn't like the man."

"Damon and I worked side by side for a couple of years, so I overheard a lot of his conversations," he began. "Crosswhite Investments has a high turnover in brokers and the only reason I made Branch Manager is that I stuck it out longer than anyone else."

"Did you ever detect in any of these conversations that someone was threatening him?" questioned Lula.

"I don't know that anyone was threatening him, but I would say that yes, there were times he was responding to someone who was angry. But we all get that from time to time."

"Does the name Oliver Jackson sound familiar?" the female detective inquired.

The young man shook his head, turning to face the computer screen on his desk. "No, but I can look it up in our system. I was given Damon's accounts after he left the firm, and it was when I started calling some of his clients that I began to sense a pattern in his dealings...Yes, Oliver Jackson. He was one of Damon's clients. I have a notation in here...several in fact...hmmm...Mister Jackson felt that he was scammed by Damon and demanded to know Damon's address. I bet I have Mister Jackson in my study."

"What study?" Frank asked.

Abbott pulled a laptop from his drawer and placed it on his desk, his fingers quickly poking at keys as he anxiously awaited the machine's response. "I don't recall all the names I deal with, so Mister Jackson's did not ring a bell right away. But he was one of Damon's clients that fit a pattern."

"A pattern for what?" Frank asked as he and Lula both stood and stepped around the desk, taking a place on either side of Abbott's chair.

"Damon would sell initial public offerings, and if the stock started to take off and had a good growth potential ahead of it, he would pressure the client to sell at a profit."

"So he was making profits for his clients," interrupted Frank. "That's not a crime."

"That's how smart he was," Abbott responded. "He would make a profit for a small investor by telling them the stock was about to tank, and then he would sell the same stock to a larger investor who held it long enough to make a larger profit. The people he screwed over often never knew they got screwed unless they continued following the value of their old stocks. And I'd guess that's why your Mister Jackson was upset."

"I don't understand," Lula said. "Why are you showing us this? Can't it hurt your company?"

Abbott reached for and held up a white envelope. "This is my resignation. My last day here is Friday. I bought a seat on the Board of Trade and come Monday, I am not looking back at this place."

"So who else has seen this?" asked Frank.

"No one," Abbott answered with a huge smile on his face. "I have to admit, I have an addiction to detective shows on television. When I started putting this together, I felt I was a detective pursuing my own investigation. But until the two of you showed up today, I really didn't think anyone else would find this very interesting."

"Is there also a pattern on who benefited on the upside of all of these transactions?" asked Frank as he pointed to the screen.

Abbott smiled. "Watch this. I am going to unhide one column of my spreadsheet with a simple click...do a quick sort...and there they are."

"Leo Salerno and a few for Wade Donovan," noted Frank as his eyes read what was on the screen.

"I hope you keep this laptop locked up in your office," Lula declared.

"No," Abbott replied. "This is my machine and it goes home with me every night."

"Did Damon get fired over this?" Frank questioned.

"Damon didn't get fired," Abbott replied. "He quit a few days after the Branch Manager at the time committed suicide."

"Suicide?" Frank reacted. "What was that guy's name?"

"Harold Klinger."

Chapter Twelve

What Frank and Lula learned from talking to Paul Abbott was not enough to charge Leo Salerno with the murder of Damon Grayson. Nor did they have any evidence from the scene that linked Salerno to Grayson's apartment on the night, at least at the very time of the murder. Nevertheless, they picked him up after leaving Crosswhite Investments and brought him to the precinct house if only to give Lieutenant Tillman the impression that they were making progress on the investigation.

Salerno played the game with them as well, not answering any of their questions until his lawyer arrived. The detectives' weak theory was dismissed as just that and Salerno was soon on his way, a few hours of his time wasted, a thousand of his dollars due to his attorney.

Frank and Lula hurriedly signed out at the end of their shift and slipped out before the Lieutenant could summon them into his office for another tongue lashing. Lula told Frank that Jamal was busy with an after school function, thus she had no reason to hurry home. After a few minutes of verbal nudging he agreed to her idea of dinner at a local restaurant not far, but then again, not close to the precinct house.

Lula's dark eyes had noticed that except for one couple, she was the only other person of her skin color in the restaurant. "Frank, does it make you feel uncomfortable to be with me because I am a black woman?"

"No, why would it?" Frank replied with surprise in this voice. "I spend all day with you. I never spent this much time in a week with my wife when I was married."

Lula leaned forward, lowering her voice. "I know. But look around you at all these other couples. Almost all of them are white. What do you think they are thinking when they look at us?"

"I don't care what they think."

"What do *you* think when you see a white woman with a black man?"

"I usually think it's none of my business," Frank answered. "And it's no one else's business if you and I are having dinner together."

"What if Molly was dating an African-American? What if she was dating Jamal?"

"I'd say that Jamal is too young for her."

"C'mon Frank," Lula pleaded. "That's not what I mean."

"Lu, I don't know what my reaction would be," he answered. "Look, I always wanted my girls to grow up and marry someone like me. And after Mary dumped me for that attorney she worked with, I feared that the girls would someday end up marrying lawyers like their stepfather. I hated the thought of that. And now that Molly is engaged to a law student, the most important thing is that she is happy."

"That's not the same thing, Frank."

"To me it is."

"Why didn't you tell me she's engaged?"

"It slipped my mind."

"How can something that important slip your mind?"

"It did."

"My sister's daughter is getting married next month," Lula announced, her fork nervously shuffling through the remnants of her dinner. "Would you like to go with me?"

Frank looked across the table into his partner's eyes, an invisible wall rapidly building before him as he replayed her words. "What's the date?"

"The 17th."

Frank squirmed in his chair fretfully, looking into the air as if there was a cue card to be found hanging from the ceiling. "I'm sorry, Lu. That day is bad for me."

Lula sat back in her chair, tilting her head to her right. "Would you have said yes if I was a white woman?"

"No, of course not," rebutted Frank.

"My race has nothing to do with it?"

"No!" asserted Frank anxiously in a low voice. "Why would you think that?"

Lula focused on her fork. Her chin tipped downward as she picked on what little remained on her plate. Frank searched across the table for her brown eyes.

"That's not true," he confessed. "The fact that you're a black woman does matter."

Lula looked up at him, surprised to hear those blunt words from Frank. She thought he was different from the majority of the other white officers she had known through the years. She often felt most of the others accepted her only because of the badge she wore.

"I need you to understand, Lu," pleaded Frank. "My personal life is a mess. I screw up everything I touch. Ever since Mary took the girls and left me, I've felt that I wasn't good enough for them, or anyone. I can't compete with their stepfather. He has the money, the looks, the career, and everything else that I can't give my girls. I can't compete with that."

"You're a good father."

"No, I'm not, Lu! I can't even help pay for Molly's wedding. I've got less than three grand in the bank and frankly, I'm worth more dead than alive. At least if I was dead, my girls would each get a hundred grand or more. I'm tired of trying to compete...and that is exactly what I would be doing if you and I got together."

"I'm just asking you to go to a wedding with me."

"Well...I've thought of more than that between us."

Lula cocked her head in further surprise as Frank continued. "You had two husbands, one that you buried and one that you kicked out. But both of them are ghosts from your past. And as a white man I could never compete with either one of them in the eyes of your family and friends. C'mon...you saw the way those guys looked at me when we were in that bar talking to Ollie Jackson."

"Frank, it's what *I* think of you what matters."

"It's not that easy, Lu. Nothing in life is that easy."

Lula tried to catch sight of Frank's eyes, but he avoided a direct glance back at her.

"I didn't know you had thought about us this much, Frank."

"Don't take this all the wrong way, Lu. Like I said, I've screwed up big time lately. I don't want to make a mess between us the way I've messed everything else."

"I shouldn't have asked you," Lula apologized. "*I'm* the one who is sorry."

Before either of them could speak the words playing in their minds, a man's voice pierced their silence from the side of the table. "How was your dinner, officers?"

"How do *you* know who we are?" Frank asked, irritated at the unwelcome intrusion.

"Your waiter told me."

"And who are you?"

"Yannis Photakas," the well-dressed stranger answered, extending his hand to Frank. "This is my restaurant."

Frank reluctantly pushed his arm upward towards that of the man, their hands clasping tightly before withdrawing back to their own bodies.

"Did you enjoy your dinner, lady?" Photakas turned to Lula, his accented words flowing smoothly from beneath a peppered mustache of silver and black.

Lula answered that she did. He thanked her and offered their dinner on the house if they would be kind enough to look at a "small problem" at the rear of the restaurant. Frank advised Photakas to call the non-emergency police number, but the restaurant owner responded that his predicament was rather urgent. Thus, Frank grudgingly agreed to the owner's request.

Lula looked at her watch. "Frank, I need to get going. I want to be there when Jamal gets home from school."

"Yeah, I'll see you tomorrow, Lu."

Frank followed Photakas through the kitchen and through a doorway leading into the alley where a gleaming, almost copper colored vehicle was parked beneath a glowing street light. No more than fourteen feet away, a scruffy looking man in long hair hung over the edge of a green garbage bin, the lid of one side pushed forward against a dark, brick wall.

"Hey, bum!" called out Photakas. As he turned, the man's dirty face was washed in the light extending to its furthermost boundary. The figure across the alley held something in his hand, which in the distance and limited light penetrating the shadows was difficult to identify, prompting Frank to place his hand inside his jacket on the butt of his holstered gun. Frank's trained eyes focused on the object and he quickly relaxed his hand. Perhaps the man was holding the leftovers of a T-bone steak, like the one Frank had just consumed. But it was not a weapon, at least not until it was thrown his way.

"He hangs around here every night," Photakas complained. "Last night he set off the alarm in my car and I *did* call the police. But by the time the officers showed up, this alley rat had already run away."

Frank glanced at the car before turning to the owner of the restaurant. "Why do you park in the alley? There is a city parking garage on the next block."

"I want to keep an eye on it."

"What did you pay for this SUV?"

"It is *not* an SUV!" Photakas answered indignantly. "This is a Sports Recreational Vehicle. I would never pay seventy-thousand dollars for an SUV."

"You paid that much for a penis extender?" Frank quickly returned. "You could have taken care of your insecurities by paying far less money to a shrink."

"I don't care to be talked to that way," Photakas replied angrily. "I am a taxpayer...and you wouldn't get paid if it wasn't for people like me."

Frank moved closer to the owner's face, a sneer upon his own, his upper teeth displayed in a show of his own resentment. "I don't care what you think. Serving and protecting doesn't include babysitting your fancy pile of sheet metal."

Frank reached into his pocket, fingered through a small fold of money and stuck a few bills in the restaurant owner's shirt pocket. "Thanks for the nice dinner, dipwad!"

Frank turned. "*You*," he called out, pointing to the little man standing at the garbage bin, "You come with me, right now."

The short man passed the restaurant owner, smiling as he looked up at him. "Dipwad!" He repeated the word several times over a deep giggle as he followed Frank out of the alley and down the street to Frank's car, where the detective opened the door and helped the stranger into the passenger seat.

"Dipwad," the passenger repeated as Frank settled behind the steering wheel. "I love that, man. I love the way you called him that. It was so cool, man."

Frank exhaled to calm himself. "Why do you keep going back there if he doesn't want you there?"

"It's my territory, man. They throw out some of the best food on the block."

"You live on the streets?"

"Yep."

Frank inhaled the odor seeping off the man's clothing; a mix of wine, cigarette smoke, and urine.

Frank started the car and drove off.

"You taking me to the slammer, man?"

"No, I'm taking you to get something to eat."

"Really?"

"Really," answered Frank. "What do they call you out here?"

"Birdy," he answered as his lips moved the hair around his mouth. "They call me Birdy 'cause I fly south for the winter. I went to Jacksonville this winter. I was in Dallas the winter before. It's better to be homeless in warm weather than in cold weather."

"You fly down, like in an airplane?" Frank asked in disbelief.

"I don't get there by flapping my arms," Birdy answered. "My daughter pays for my plane ticket there and back."

"Is your daughter the reason you come back to Chicago?"

Birdy laughed. "No, man. My daughter lives in St. Louis."

"Then why do you come back to Chicago?"

"'Cause I like it here, man."

Frank powered the windows down on both sides of the car to flush out the odor reeking from the man's clothing. "What is your real name, Birdy?"

"Frank," he answered. "But that was in my other life."

"Frank is my name, too."

Birdy gave out a deep laugh to the detective's reply. "You wanna trade lives?"

"No," Frank shook his head, glancing over to his bearded passenger. "What do you want to eat, Birdy? Your choices are hot dogs, Italian Beef, pizza, or hamburgers."

"Oh, hamburgers," Birdy blurted out. "No one ever throws away a good hamburger. Would it be okay if I had a cheeseburger?"

"Sure," Frank smiled.

Frank picked up a couple of cheeseburgers with fries and a chocolate shake and dropped Birdy off at a nearby park, handing him ten dollars for spending money. He knew that Birdy would end up returning to that garbage dumpster behind the restaurant for his next meal, but for now—for now Frank did what made him feel good.

He had driven about two blocks and was at a stop light when he recognized a Hispanic man among three who were entering a corner liquor store. Frank parked his car and walked to the corner, leaning his back on the brightly lit window as he waited. A few minutes went by before the three men exited the store and began to walk past Frank.

"Hey, Vega," Frank called out. "I heard you were paroled."

The three men turned sharply to face Frank. Vega was the shorter of the three, and the larger in bulk. His head was shaven, and diamonds glimmered from both of his ear lobes. A newly lit cigarette dangled from his lips as the tattoo of a snake crawled out of his white tee shirt and up the side of his neck.

The two other men closed ranks with him as Vega spoke to them in Spanish. "Well, well, well...I thought I would have to find *you*, McKay. But here you are. And all alone, I see."

"I heard you told the parole board that you *weren't* looking for me," Frank retaliated.

"I had to tell them what they wanted to hear."

"So you haven't changed your mind about me?"

Vega turned his head and continued speaking Spanish to the two men with him, but Frank interrupted him mid-sentence. "That's the coward's way out, Vega...speaking Spanish so I can't hear. Are you that afraid of me?"

Vega clinched his teeth and lowered his brow in anger. "This is the cop who killed my little brother. That's what I started telling my friends here."

"Why don't you tell them the whole story?"

"The whole story is that you killed Miguel."

"You just can't accept your part in it...can you, Vega?"

As Vega stepped forward Frank did also, placing his hand inside his jacket on the handle of his gun. Vega backed off, and then turned around, pointing his finger at Frank. "I told my mother that I was sorry. I told Miguel I was sorry. *You* never told any of us that you were sorry."

"So you still want to kill me, Vega?"

Vega stared at Frank, but he didn't answer.

Frank moved closer to Vega, towering over him with his height. "You know what I think? I think you haven't got the guts to kill me. Miguel had the guts. But *you*, with your shiny little head and pretty earrings, you're just an advertisement that you aren't man enough to back up your big mouth."

Vega shouted back. "I can kill you. But I don't have a weapon on me. You wanna search us, cop? None of us have weapons. I'll kill you. I swear on my brother's grave that I'll kill you."

Frank stood his ground, his feet firmly set on the cement of the Chicago sidewalk. "Oh, Vega...if your parole officer knew you were talking this way, he'd have your ass on the next bus back to where you came from."

"I hate you, cop!" snarled Vega in return.

Frank pulled a business card from his pocket, quickly writing on the blank back side. He stepped forward, sticking the card down Vega's shirt. "That's my card...with my cell phone and home address. I'm not afraid of you, Luis. You'll never be half the man that Miguel was."

Frank turned into the stripes of light and shadow beneath the glowing street lamps, listening to the raised voices of the three men throwing obscenities his way in English and Spanish. His heart raced rapidly, outpacing the rhythm of his shoes against the hard surface of the sidewalk below. He didn't look back until he reached the door of his car. Vega and the two others were gone. Frank's clothes and hair were brushed with the warmed air pushed aside by the traffic behind him until he was safely inside where he leaned back, closed his eyes, and took a deep breath.

Chapter Thirteen

Frank squeezed the emptiness from the chair next to Sal Martin's desk as he carefully placed a covered paper cup in front of the bald officer. "Vega has the same haircut as you, Sal."

"You saw him?"

"Last night."

"Did he see you?"

"Yeah, we had a nice little talk."

Sal leaned over, his elbow pressing atop the armrest as he swiveled his chair. His eyes scanned the length from Frank's face down to his shoes. "Well, you look like you're in one piece."

"Yeah, the little creep isn't going to do anything."

Sal carefully pried the little triangle of plastic off the white cover, dipping his head down to the opening. He drew a small amount of the hot, dark liquid between his lips, savoring the feel and taste as it moved over his tongue and down his throat. "Hmmm...I can taste why they charge three bucks a cup for this stuff. Thanks, Frank."

"You're just use to what they flush out of that vending machine," Frank nodded. "I got your message. What do you have?"

"A couple of things, my friend," Sal began. "I sent Schwack and Coomer back to the crime scene after your visit with Doctor Epson. Short of tearing down the walls, they didn't find anything that we missed the first time."

"What about those tapes and DVDs at the scene?"

"We thought your victim may have disguised them as legit movies, so Coomer brought them back here and took a look at the whole collection. Every last one was as marked. He's got some popcorn left over in the conference room."

Frank shook his head. "Lu and I checked to see if Grayson had a safe deposit box or a storage locker, but we've come up empty on those."

"What about this other guy—Salerno?"

"I don't think so," doubted Frank. "He seemed real antsy to get into Grayson's apartment, though my gut tells me it has more to do with their business dealings. I don't know if he's aware of Grayson's blackmailing scheme. And if he does, I don't think he has a clue where the tapes may be."

"Can you get a warrant to search his place?"

Frank shook his head. "We don't have enough on him. Briggs and I questioned him at his place and then hauled him down to our house for a second round, but we didn't get any bad vibes off the guy. And to tell you the truth, Sal...if I went to Tillman asking for a search warrant for Salerno's place, he'd kick me out of his office."

"By the way, where is Briggs?"

"She called in sick. I don't think her dinner went down that well last night."

"Well, we went over Grayson's computer again, and it's clean. We found some spreadsheets, but nothing indicating business dealings; and no lists of names or addresses. He had a file of photos, but those were no different than what I keep on mine of the wife and kids."

"We're missing something on this guy. But even if we could figure out who else Grayson was blackmailing," Frank confided, "That only gives us motive. We still don't have anything leading us to the shooter."

"Maybe we do," Sal smiled. "We got a hit on one of the sets of prints that Coomer lifted off the door, the television, a paperweight that we found *inside* the computer's smashed monitor, and in the kitchen."

"Yeah, whose are they?"

"Gunnar Ingolf Nordhagen," Sal replied. "His address for the last six months has been Minneapolis, Minnesota. And for the three years prior to that, he has had an all expenses paid vacation courtesy of the Minnesota Correctional System."

"Was he paroled?"

"Yes, so unless Grayson's apartment took a ride up to Minnesota, this Gunnar fellow was violating his parole."

"What was he in for?"

Sal flipped a sheet of paper around and positioned it on his desktop in front of Frank. "Domestic assault...physical abuse of his wife and kids...and they even tacked on a couple of years for resisting arrest and assault because he sent a cop to the hospital."

"Well, there must be some tie in to Grayson," Frank wondered. "I may have to pay my friend Salerno another visit after all."

Frank's cell phone rang. "Yeah, this is McKay... yeah, I know him...what hospital...I'll be there in thirty minutes."

"What's up?" Sal asked.

"A guy Lu and I talked to yesterday was robbed last night. He's over at Swedish Covenant hospital."

Chapter Fourteen

The detective from robbery division who made the call to Frank was waiting outside Paul Abbott's hospital room.

"Are you McKay?" he asked.

"Yeah, what happened?"

"The victim was attacked and robbed last night. He was out for awhile...we didn't get the call until about four this morning. It's clearly a robbery, but he insisted on talking to you. He said you interviewed him yesterday in a murder investigation?"

"Yeah, the Grayson case," Frank answered. "How is he?"

"The doctors are keeping him here for observation, but he should be fine. It took a dozen or so stitches to close his head wound."

"Does this fit the pattern of anything else you've got going?" Frank inquired.

"No," the other detective answered. "The description is sketchy; black ski mask, black gloves, and a bulky coat or vest...which for this time of year seemed a bit strange."

"What's missing?"

"His wallet...about a hundred bucks, give or take... and his computer," the robbery detective read from his notes.

"Was it a laptop?"

The other detective gave an affirmative nod of his head, "Does that mean something?"

"Abbott had files on that machine that might be related to our murder case. Then again, it might just be coincidence."

"I need to get back on the street," the other detective said. "I was just sticking around until you got here."

"Yeah, thanks," uttered Frank as he turned and quietly entered Abbott's room. Abbott was in the room alone, in the bed next to a window, the view from which was a panorama of rooftops interrupted by sporadic outcrops of green crowns. Abbott was propped up against a fluffy white pillow, his eyes closed until he heard Frank's footsteps. He pushed a smile to his face as he recognized the visitor from homicide. "Hi, Detective...you heard the news."

"Yeah, Paul," Frank replied. "I got here as soon as I could. How are you doing?"

"I have a super ache across my head, and when I start my new job next week, I'm gonna look like I've been in a bar fight."

Frank stood at the foot of Abbott's bed, eyeing the white dressing wrapped around the injured man's forehead. "When did this happen?"

"About nine last night...I know because I was getting ready to watch one of my detective shows. I had been sitting on my couch getting some work done on my laptop. That's when the guy knocked on my door."

"How do you know it was a man?"

"What?" Abbott asked in return. "I don't know. He had a mask over his head and he looked muscular."

"Did this guy say anything to you?"

"He didn't say a word. He just pointed a gun to my forehead and put his finger over his mouth... you know...like this." Abbott held his finger over his mouth in the common gesture that librarians use in controlling voice levels in the presence of deaf books. "Then he did one of these," Abbott gestured with a slicing, horizontal motion across his neck.

"Was there anything about him that you remember?"

"He was African-American or Hispanic. I could see through the holes in his mask that his eyes and the skin around them were brown."

"What did he do next?"

"He patted the back of my pants...looking for my wallet I guess. Then he walked me into my bedroom. When he saw my wallet on top of the dresser...he grabbed it, swung me around, and hit me in the back of the head."

"And he took your laptop?"

"That's why I asked to see you," Abbott answered. "I thought it could have something to do with your case."

"Maybe it is, Paul," Frank smiled. "Can you do one more thing for me?"

"Sure."

"I'm going to send over another detective with a book on handguns. Do you think you might recognize the gun from a picture?"

"I doubt it. I was too scared to move my eyes off his ski mask. I'm sorry."

"Give it a try anyway," Frank responded. "And from now on you'd better ask who's at the door before you open it. If you think of anything else, give me a call. But for now, get some sleep while I go after some of the bad guys out there."

Part of Frank told him what happened to Abbott was nothing more than coincidence. Then again, the victim was a man clearly fascinated, if not borderline obsessed, by detective shows. Perhaps he staged the so-called robbery to gain Frank and Lula's attention. Frank's gut also nagged him to consider the unthinkable, but he shook off the perverted notion. He didn't want to believe that he could possibly know Abbott's assailant.

Frank always saw the irony that there was little growing green on Greenview Avenue in Chicago's Bucktown, where his brother Mickey lived in a small apartment. The creak echoed through the hallway from each ancient stair pressed beneath the soles of Frank's shoes as he stepped up to the second floor. The frosted window on the bathroom door shared by both apartments on the same floor glowed softly from the sunlight filtering through the small window inside. Frank remembered life in this very same building, having lived there seven, maybe eight years with his parents and brother when he was a kid.

The door to Mickey's apartment was unlocked, just as Frank's brother left it most of the time. Frank no longer bothered to make the wasted effort to tell his brother to fasten the bolt each night. It was a futile suggestion, even though Frank felt he had the right to voice his opinion if he wished. It was Frank who paid the monthly rent. He couldn't trust Mickey to make the payments because his brother would rather drink or gamble away the money for rent or any other bills. Frank tried trusting his brother once or twice or three times—he had lost count. But Mickey ended up on the streets—like Birdy. Frank also paid half of what it took to keep their father in a nursing home; though he never expected the old man's heart to continue beating for as long as it had.

Mickey was still sprawled out, fully dressed atop the untidy blankets on his bed. "Mickey, wake up!" Frank called out. "It's your big brother Frank."

Mickey moaned and turned his face away from Frank, his eyes still closed.

"Wake up, Mickey!" Frank raised his voice, piercing through his brother's sleep again. "I need to talk to you."

Frank walked back into the kitchen and to the refrigerator, opening and then closing the door quickly before a pungent odor succeeded in its attempt to escape. He leaned over the kitchen sink and tried to look through the glass of a window filmed in dust. Just as well, Frank thought as he created a diagonal line with the tip of his finger. After all, the view beyond the dust was nothing more than the same block of brown bricks that had been there forever. Twenty-two in all inside the imaginary boundary of the window frame. The number was imbedded in Frank's memory. He had counted those same bricks again and again while standing in that very same spot as a kid, washing dishes as punishment.

"What time is it?" Mickey asked as he returned from a visit to the narrow space between apartments.

"It's noon, Mickey," Frank glanced over his shoulder. "The living world has already been awake for four hours."

Mickey's yellowish fingers sorted through an overfilled ashtray on the metal kitchen table top until he found a cigarette butt with a quarter-inch of white paper exposed from a tan filter. He lifted it to his mouth and then pushed both of his open hands into his side pockets until one came out grasping a book of matches.

"Can you lend me money so I can buy some smokes?" he asked, a light gray cloud rolling out of his nostrils, his sandy hair reaching in every direction at once.

Frank walked over to the table and dropped a twenty dollar bill in front of his brother.

"Thanks, Frank," Mickey responded to the green bill. "I'll pay you back when I get my welfare check."

"Forget it, Mickey. You never pay me back... why do you even bother to say that?"

"Hey, don't kick a man when he's down."

"I need to talk to you about something."

"What? Did the old man finally kick the bucket?"

"No," denied Frank. "It's about my insurance policy and my will."

"What about it?"

"I'm changing them. I want Molly and Megan to be the beneficiaries on my policy and I'm naming Molly as the executor on my will."

"Why the hell would you do that, Frank?" Mickey looked up at him. "Don't you trust me any longer?"

"What? Do I think that you could possibly drink or piss away the money before my daughters saw a dime of it? Yeah, the thought crossed my mind." Frank sat down next to Mickey upon a rickety chair with rust blemished legs. He pushed away the ashtray to the other side of the table. "But that's not the reason, Mickey. I had your name on all my papers because I didn't want Mary to get any of it if I got killed on the job or died."

"So what the hell has changed that you want to do this?"

"Because Molly is old enough to handle the responsibility," Frank answered. "And it's my way of connecting with her again."

"C'mon Frank, that's all a bunch of BS! What about me and the old man? Are you throwing us out on the street because you want to be nicey-nicey with your kid?"

"No, Mickey," answered Frank, "I've got it all worked out in my head. Nothing changes. I'm going to include in the new will that Dad's nursing home is paid for as long as he is alive. And of course I'll make sure you're covered. You're my brother."

"What do Molly and Megan get?"

"I'm changing my insurance policy to give two hundred grand to Molly with the other one-twenty for Megan," explained Frank. "But paying for you and Dad would come out of Molly's share."

"Who gets it all now?"

"You do. But the current will stipulates that you would give Molly and Megan a hundred grand each and you would pay for you and Dad out of the remaining one-twenty."

"And you think because I'm a bum that I can't do what you want me to do?"

"Yeah...no...yeah...c'mon Mickey, this isn't about you," answered Frank in frustration. "When

I did this in the first place you had a job and were trying to turn your life around...look at this place... look at yourself."

"I'm sorry that we all can't be like you, Frank."

The table shook on its weak legs as Frank pushed himself up from the chair. He exhaled his frustration through his nose as he turned away from his brother. "I came here because you are my only family. Who else is there? That SOB that we call our father doesn't recognize either one of us any longer. Why can't you just hear me out instead of looking for the dollar signs?"

"Does Molly even know I exist?" Mickey asked. "I haven't seen her in years."

"You don't need to worry about getting your share. It's not like I'm going to die tomorrow."

After sucking out the last remaining trace of smoke in the cigarette butt held firmly between his fingers, Mickey rubbed it out and immediately began searching for a replacement among the gray ash.

"When are you making all these changes?"

"A couple of weeks."

"Do I need to do anything?"

"No."

"Then I guess that's that," Mickey looked up.

Frank took another twenty out of his pocket and dropped it across the other bill lying flat between his brother's outstretched arms. And with neither man saying another word, Frank turned his back and closed the door, the stale air creaking from each downward stair pressed beneath his shoes.

Chapter Fifteen

Frank was on his own with Lula off for the day, providing him the opportunity to stop by Vince's house and talk over the case with his previous partner. Frank and Vince functioned well together. Neither of them hesitated to bounce ad-hoc ideas or theories of their investigations off the other. It wasn't just a matter of each feeling they could speak what was developing in their minds. They both knew what they said was being heard and considered. Frank missed that connection.

He and Lula were coworkers and friends, but they had not yet melded into each other's personality as Frank and Vince had done. And Frank would not suggest a visit with Vince to talk over the case if Lula was with him. Vince listened as Frank talked, soon comfortable with the subject that his friend had brought with him in the unexpected visit.

"I don't know, Vince," Frank finished. "That's what we've got up to now. What would you do next?"

"I'd go back to the scene and start over again," Vince answered without pause. "I know how your mind works, Frank. If Sal and his team missed anything, you'll pick it up."

"I guess that can't hurt."

Vince was pleased with his own response to Frank, but turned the subject to something else that had more momentum on his mind. "Have you heard anything about my status?"

"Isn't Tillman keeping you up to date?"

"Are you kidding? He hasn't bothered to call me since the first week I was in the...you know... place."

Frank stalled for a long moment, not sure whether he wanted to deflate the sudden rise in Vince's mood. But there was no need to add little lies to the large lie Frank kept secret. "Pete Richter stopped over at the precinct to see me. He said it isn't looking good for you and suggested that you hire a lawyer."

"You mean I've got to fight to get my job back?"

"I guess."

The door opened and Vince dropped the subject from his mind and pushed up quickly from his recliner as his eyes turned towards the entrance. It was Angie, carrying two brown paper bags, groceries peeking out of the openings of their tops. Vince met her, retrieved the packages and vanished promptly into the kitchen.

"Frank, what are *you* doing here?" Angie asked, pulling at the strands of her hair to set them in place.

"I thought you'd be at work today."

"I was this morning, but took the afternoon off to do some shopping."

Vince reentered the room, asking his wife if there were any more bags to be brought into the house.

"No," she answered. "But Vince, I am really worried about the car. I kept hearing a loud rattling sound from the back while I was driving."

"I'll look at it later."

"Can you please look at it now before I go out shopping again," she pleaded. "I don't want to get stuck on the street somewhere."

Vince reluctantly agreed before turning to Frank. "But I don't want you to go anywhere yet. The two of you are the only people in my life who I can trust and it feels good to have you in the same room together."

Angie held the door open, watching anxiously as Vince started her car, and then got out again, circling the vehicle, his ears listening for the reported sound. He motioned towards the open door that he couldn't hear anything, returned to the car, and pulled away from the curb to begin his test drive. Angie closed the door and turned to Frank, his own gaze fixed out the front window while his fingers held back the edge of the curtains.

"I have missed you so much, Frank," Angie said with emotion seeping into each word as she moved towards him.

"Don't, Angie," he warned with his hand held up between them. "Please, we talked about this and agreed it had to end."

"But I can't stop thinking about you," she pleaded as her body drew closer, the wake trailing her words brushing Frank's senses. "I never felt so alive in my life as when I was in your arms. I know it was wrong, but you and I are meant to be with one another. Why can't you see that?"

Frank nervously braced his stare through the clear of the window as the surface of his skin and the air drawn through his nostrils savored her presence. "We can't, Angie. If Vince found out, it would destroy him. I'm so sorry...I should never have kissed you that night. I should have stopped it then."

"But I love you, Frank," she continued to beg with the eyes Frank avoided. "And no matter what you say, I know you love me. I read your cards and letters and..."

"You still have those?" Frank asked with panic in his voice. "You said you would get rid of those, Ange."

"I can't...they are all I have left of you."

"Angie, you've got to throw those away! If Vince found them, he'd know everything." Frank peeked back through the curtains. "Damn it! He's back."

Like two hormone incited teenagers about to be caught by one of their parents, Angie ran to the kitchen and Frank rushed back to the couch, forcing a look of pleasant surprise as Vince opened the front door.

"I don't hear anything in her car," Vince announced as he came in from his short excursion.

Frank bounced back up from the couch, his nerves rushing heat to his skin. "Vince, I really need to get going. Tillman is on my back the way it is, and I haven't done much today to move this case along. But I am definitely going to follow your advice and check out Grayson's apartment again."

Frank wondered if Vince could feel the aura of emotion left drifting in the room—the energy that sparked between Frank and Angie and threatened to push them into a stolen embrace in the moments before his return. Frank's straining resistance could not have held much longer against the temptation to pull Angie close to him once again; to touch the smallness of her figure in his arms, to taste and smell and feel the softness of her lips against his. He trembled inside at the thought of Vince finding the cards and letters that Angie had not thrown away; greeting cards of support and friendship and the most fearsome being those that contained the dangerous word "love". One could excuse the others as being supportive, but only a fool would accept the hint of another man's real love for his wife. And the few letters that Frank wrote in his handwriting were no less damaging, because the words could not hide the undercurrent of love for the woman whose name was at the top of the first page, by the man whose name was on the bottom of the last. Vince would never understand. He could never be expected to accept the part of Frank's final letter confessing that his affair with Angie was wrong. All that would matter is what they had done together—to him.

Chapter Sixteen

Frank's knock on the door was answered by a short, overweight woman whose unnaturally colored hair was wrapped around large pink curlers, most of which were hidden beneath a blue scarf. He averted his eyes as they realized the material of her lime green moo-moo was translucent and Frank had no desire to confirm his initial suspicion that the woman had no underwear above her waist.

"I'm Detective McKay," Frank announced with a flash of his ID. "I'm looking for the building manager."

"He ain't here, Honey," she answered in a smoky voice. "He's at the hardware store. What do you need?"

"The key to Damon Grayson's apartment."

"Which one?"

"The one to the front door."

"Which one, Honey?"

"How many front doors does he have?" Frank asked, confused by the exchange.

"Two," she answered. "He had two apartments. The one in which he was killed, and the one above it. So which one will it be, Honey?"

"Both...I'll take both...why didn't your husband tell us about the other apartment?"

The woman shrugged her shoulders. "Probably 'cause no one asked him, Honey. You'll have to ask *him.*"

Frank slipped the key into the slot, turning it until a faint click signaled him to turn the brass knob and push the door inward into the still apartment. The glow from a dim bulb in the hallway behind him cast a diagonal shadow down the wall where a light switch sat on the borderline between the unlit and lit surface of a dark blue wall. With one hand on the butt of his gun and one finger loosely resting on the trigger, he flipped the switch with his other hand, illuminating two standing lamps in the room before him.

"Police!" he called out. "Is anyone here?"

The silence answered back that he was alone and Frank closed the door, stepping forward slowly as he surveyed the sparsely furnished room before him. The two tall lamps on long stems of dark brown flanked a turquoise chair that faced a television on a stand on the opposite wall. Frank flicked another switch that turned on a light on the ceiling of a hallway leading to the kitchen on the far end. Mimicking the floor plan of the apartment below, two closed doors marked the entrance to two rooms, one on each side of the narrow connecting the room in front and the kitchen.

Frank slowly opened and pushed the door to the room above that of Jennifer Goodman one floor down. Slanting lines of daylight filtered through a curtainless window, pointing to a large oval carpet in the center of the floor. A black cable protruded from the brown oval on the opposite side of the room, drawing the detective's curiosity. He stooped, propped up shakily by the heel of one shoe. Lifting a pair of latex gloves from his pocket, he pulled them over his hands before raising the edge of the ridged floor covering. His fingers and eyes followed the direction of the cables, to the wall, and then up to a desk to an idle VCR recorder, its power light bright red in forgetfulness.

Frank rolled the edges of the carpet until one end of the cable dropped into a hole near the center of the floor. He hurriedly pushed himself to his feet, out the front door, down the stairs to the next floor down, and into the apartment below. Above Jennifer's bed was a mirror, a rectangle roughly two feet by four, dropping from the ceiling in a frame two inches in height. Frank stood upon Jennifer's bed and ran his fingers around the edges of the frame, seeking a latch or some other easy way of removing the mirror.

"Screw it!" he said aloud to the emptiness around him. He pulled the handgun from its holster, covered his face with his jacket, and with the butt facing upward, he shattered the mirror with one hard whack. The glass rained down upon and past him, resting on the mattress and carpet below. Facing down at him in the opening created above was the camera to which the cable led.

Frank returned to the apartment above, to the room where the recordings were made. He scanned the area between the four walls, but there were no dressers, no cabinets, no bookcases, and no trace of video tapes.

As he turned the knob on the door to the room across the hall, it quickly held. Frank ran his fingers over the edge of the trim above the door in search of a key, but his touch found nothing. He inspected the walls in the kitchen and the top and insides of a sparsely filled refrigerator. He looked inside the kitchen's cabinet doors. He peeked under and ran his hands over the bottom of the wall cabinets. He pulled each horizontal drawer open, then quickly shoved each closed as his eyes searched for any key that he could try in the lock. But he found nothing. The key had to be in the apartment below, if not among the evidence taken by Sal Martin and his team.

But Frank no longer wanted to waste his time searching. He lowered his shoulder and banged into the door hard and banged into it again harder and harder once more until it was pushed inward from his determination. Even before he flicked the wall switch up, his eyes found what his gut told him was there. The computer, black screened monitor, and printer sat neatly in place on an L-shaped desk. An unopened package of video tapes was almost perfectly aligned along the back edge of the top of the desk. Frank pulled out the wheeled chair tucked beneath the desk and sat down. He slowly opened a drawer on his right. The name "Harold Klinger" looked up at him from a white label fastened along the edge of the first of a long row of video tapes. Lined up neatly next to Klinger's tape were more, with each label bearing the names of men in the same printing. Some names appeared on more than one tape. The names of Kale Epson and Wade Donovan were the two other names recognized by Frank as he copied them into his notebook. But missing from the row of labels was the name of Gunnar Nordhagen, whose fingerprints had been found in Grayson's apartment.

Frank walked back to the room into which he entered the apartment and placed the tape of Doctor Epson into the VCR machine, turned on the television and pressed the play button. The tapes did not reveal Grayson as a filmmaker by profession, but they were clear enough to identify the faces of the Doctor and Jennifer atop the naked bodies meshed together. And if the date and time fixed in the lower right hand corner of the screen image was correct, then Jennifer was not old enough to do what she was doing, or more important legally, what was being done to her.

Frank spent the hours that followed viewing each tape long enough to identify Jennifer as the female in all but one. For each tape he wrote the name and description of the man and the dates imprinted on the screen. The same video tape often showed multiple encounters of the man named on the tape with Jennifer. And as he continued to watch, Frank realized that neither girl was innocent. They clearly called out each man's name several times, and were careful to keep the backs of their own heads from blocking the faces of the men from the camera's view when they positioned the unsuspecting men on their backs. In the one tape in which Jennifer was not the female participant, Wade Donovan bounced around with a young girl of blonde hair who did not look older than fourteen. That tape had the most recent date of those Frank recorded in his notes, stamped with a date just seven months prior to the murder of Grayson. That was one of three tapes of Donovan, two of which were of him with Jennifer. The tapes were the reason Donovan offered to get robbery involved in the investigation.

The names on the tapes also added to Frank's list of suspects, with the exception of the deceased Harold Klinger. He sat there thinking hours into the night before he reached a decision. He found a black, plastic garbage bag beneath the kitchen sink and used it carry the entire collection of Grayson's tapes to the trunk of his car in the cover of the evening dark. He held the trunk down with the palms of both hands, his eyes closed as he gave himself one more chance to change his mind.

Chapter Seventeen

"My attorney told me not to talk to the police without him being present," Leo Salerno told Frank through the narrow opening in his doorway after he responded to the hard knock.

"I understand," Frank responded with a faint smirk pushed across his tired face. "Why don't you and your lawyer meet me down at the precinct and we can talk about these tapes I found." Frank held one tape to meet Salerno's eye level.

"Please come in," Salerno answered, pulling the door inward. "No partner today?"

"No. Where is Jennifer?"

"She is at a singing lesson," replied Salerno with his eyes on the tape. "Where did you find this?"

"You don't know?"

"No."

Salerno's magnified eyes grew larger with surprise as Frank tossed the tape in his direction. The tape tumbled between Salerno's hands for a fraction of seconds before his fingers tamed it in their grasp. "Who is Harold Klinger?" he asked, reading the label.

Frank studied Salerno's face. "You really don't know who he is, do you?"

"No."

"But you knew about the tapes. Right?"

"Wade Donovan told me about *his* tape the week before Damon died," Salerno answered. "And after you and your partner left the other day, Jennifer told me there were probably other tapes as well."

Salerno moved over to his chair, placing the tape on the low table in front of him as he sat.

"Leo, do you expect me to believe that you weren't in on this with Grayson?"

"I wasn't. I had my suspicions, but even though Damon was my business partner, the subject of Jennifer was delicate."

"Can you give me a name for the other girl?"

"What other girl?"

"All but one of the tapes I found starred Jennifer. But the most recent tape showed your pal Donovan with a younger girl...a blonde...and according to the date on the video, that little escapade was filmed just seven months ago."

"Seven months ago?"

"Stop the stalling tactic, Leo! You expect me to believe you don't know anything that went on?"

"I never met this other girl," Salerno answered. "Damon asked if she could stay with me, but I told him no. I suggested that he let Jennifer live here instead, but as always, he was against *that* idea. And it was a moot point anyway because this other girl took off soon afterward."

"What do mean...she *left*?"

"Yes."

"Do you know why?"

"No."

"Do you know her name?"

"Jennifer told me her name was Erin," replied Salerno. "But that is all I know. As I said, Detective, I never met this other girl."

"Tell me, Leo," Frank continued. "Why weren't you in any of those tapes?"

Salerno looked away as he answered. "Jennifer and I didn't have that kind of relationship."

"Do you feel you missed out?"

Salerno turned his eyes towards Frank briefly before turning away again. "No," he said softly.

"Leo, I know about the stock scam you and Grayson were running."

"That was not a scam, as you call it," rebutted Salerno. "Damon sold me stocks in legitimate transactions. And I turned many of them around for good profit margins."

"And I bet some of those profits found their way into Grayson's pockets," contested Frank.

"I am a Certified Public Accountant, Detective. If what you are saying is true, do you think it would be possible for anyone to prove such an outlandish allegation?"

"You're right, Leo. How can I be so stupid to even think such a thing. How can I be so stupid to believe anything coming out of your mouth?"

"No one here is calling you stupid, Detective. As a matter of fact, I sense that you are quite intelligent."

Frank and Salerno stared at one another, each anticipating the other to speak next.

"Why did Wade Donovan come to you, Leo?" Frank asked, ending the momentary waiting game. "That part doesn't make sense to me. If Grayson was blackmailing Donovan, why come to you?"

Leo stood from his chair without answering, walking over to a couch table where he picked up a small bottle of lens cleaner. He removed his glasses from his face, sprayed twice, and returned to his seat while wiping the liquid off his thick lenses. With his glasses held in his hands, his squinting eyes looked unnaturally small.

"I didn't know about the tapes," he stated. "I knew that Damon was more persuasive than I was in our business dealings with others. We bought real estate together at prices that I thought were unrealistically low, from men who seemed at first reluctant to deal."

"And you didn't suspect that Grayson was doing something immoral, if not illegal?"

"The only thing I needed to know was that Damon was an excellent deal maker and that I was an excellent accountant who provided the capital."

"Was it real estate with Donovan as well?" Frank asked, "Or was it city contracts?"

"Neither," Salerno answered. "With Donovan it was all about favors. After his brother became Mayor, Donovan was given the position of negotiating with movie producers when they sought to film in Chicago. Damon pressured Donovan to arrange for Jennifer to get a small part in a movie. She was thrilled, so Damon pressured Donovan for another movie, and that one turned into a few lines of dialogue. And surprisingly, she did quite well."

"I still don't understand why Donovan came to you."

"Because of Jennifer," Salerno answered back. "Jennifer left Damon and came to live with me, and Damon went to Donovan threatening to release the tapes to the media if Donovan didn't convince me to send Jennifer back."

"And with the Mayor getting ready for a run as Governor, Donovan freaked out?"

"Yes, and there are millions of dollars at stake for both of the Donovan brothers."

Frank clasped his hands together and tapped his forehead several times as he connected the dots of logic in everything he had gathered thus far since the beginning of the investigation. "Leo, tell me about this relationship between Jennifer and Grayson and you. She was just a teenager in most of the tapes that I found."

Salerno's body fidgeted uneasily in his chair. "Damon found her living on the street. I didn't realize until much later that she was a runaway and not Damon's niece as he originally told me. Damon's children were grown and I never had any myself...so when Jennifer started calling us Uncle Damon and Uncle Leo, it was special to both of us. We spoiled her to no end."

"Damon abused her, Leo."

"I know that now," Salerno confessed. "But Jennifer has a way of getting what she wants. She knew how to push both of our buttons, so to speak. And we in turn sent her to the best school, bought her the most expensive clothes, and gave her everything and anything that she wanted."

"Did she live with both of you?"

"No. She stayed with me for a day or two from time to time, but Damon always found a reason to cut her time with me short. And when the time came for her to escape from Damon, she knew she was welcome here."

"So why did she move out of Grayson's place?"

"She got tired of being used. Damon was afraid he would lose her if she pursued acting and I saw their disagreement as my way of getting Jennifer to move in with me. So I told her that I would support her career if she left Damon. And she did."

"So who is using who now, Leo? If she got tired of Damon, don't you think she'll get tired of you if this acting thing works out for her?"

"I try not to think of that."

"I don't know, Leo," said Frank. "It sure sounds to me like both you and Donovan had your own motives to kill Grayson."

"I told you that I didn't kill him!" Salerno insisted.

"Hey, calm down," Frank replied. "I said you both had your motives. I'm not accusing you of his murder. At least not yet."

"What do you want from me, Detective?"

"Just some straight answers for once," Frank answered.

Frank looked back at Salerno's lens-enlarged eyes, searching for some indication of the truth.

"Leo, who is Gunnar Nordhagen?"

"I...I don't know," Leo stuttered.

"By your reaction, I think you do. That name hit a raw nerve there."

Salerno crossed his arms over his chest, dropping his chin momentarily before lifting his head up once again. "I grew up in the Bridgeport neighborhood when Comiskey Park was still called Comiskey Park. Nordhagen was the name of a leftfielder for the White Sox at one time...that's why I recognized the name."

"Oh c'mon, Leo! Do you really expect me to fall for a lame explanation like that?"

"Believe what you want to believe, Detective. I never met anyone named Gunnar Nordhagen."

Before Frank could respond, Salerno asked a question in return. "What are you going to do with the rest of the tapes?"

"They're evidence," Frank answered. "I'll turn them over to the DA when I'm done with them."

"Is that really necessary?" articulated Salerno.

"What are you getting at, Leo?"

Salerno's response had to wait until he thought about the words he was about to say, if he dared say them at all. "Those tapes didn't kill Damon."

"Yeah, but one of the men on those tapes may be the man I'm after."

Salerno leaned forward slowly. "Within a few thousand dollars either way, I know how much money you make in a year, Detective. And I know your pension isn't nearly as much as you would like."

"Be careful, Leo," Frank warned.

Leo held up two hands, his palms opened. "I am just talking...that's all. I am just saying that those tapes are probably worth three to four times what you make in a year."

Frank placed his hand on the tape on the table and pulled it up with him as he stood. "This guy Klinger took his own life. I think the innocent men on those tapes would live easier if the rest of these were destroyed."

"You wouldn't do that, would you?"

"Why? Why would you want them, Leo? Do you want to pick up where Damon left off? Blackmail is a crime...as is bribery."

Salerno shrugged his shoulders. "This is just an innocent discussion, Detective. It's nothing more than that."

Nothing more, Salerno said. But Frank left Salerno's place replaying the man's words. If it was an offer—why not? Why not give Salerno the tapes for what would amount to between a hundred and two hundred thousand. That kind of money would go a long way at the right time to ease the financial worries working his mind. He could contribute to Molly's wedding and give her money towards a house. Why should Molly's rich step-father and her mother overshadow Frank again? He had been a honest cop his entire career and look where it got him—his life had flat-lined long ago and he felt trapped in a hole with no escape. Vince was a good cop *and* a good man and look what it got *him*—the department was ready to sacrifice Corelli for what? To save face? To protect an image? Loyalty was no longer a two-way deal in the department, so why should Frank worry about one little side agreement. After all, the tapes weren't a murder weapon—they weren't part of the crime scene. How many times had he and Vince risked their lives arresting criminals just to have the dirt bags buy their way out of being convicted?

He went to Salerno's place looking for answers, but left haunted by the questions planted by the man's responses.

Chapter Eighteen

Frank marched briskly through the busy squad room, ignoring the looks and verbal greetings of those officers who noticed him as he passed by their desks. He pushed open the half-closed door to the Lieutenant's office and placed a single video tape on Tillman's desk.

"What is this, McKay?"

"It's your pal Donovan having fun with a girl under the legal age for consent. This is the reason he wanted you to get robbery involved in Grayson's murder."

"Where did you get this?"

"It turns out that our dead guy had two apartments, one right above the other," explained Frank, glaring downward from the front of the Lieutenant's desk.

"Did you have a warrant?"

"Did I need one? This was an extension of the crime scene," Frank argued. "Besides, this is sensitive stuff. I thought you'd want to see it before anyone else knew about it. Did I do the wrong thing?"

The Lieutenant recognized the defiance in Frank's voice, but chose to avoid the challenge. He was weary of the recent friction and verbal sparing that had aggravated his ulcer. In his mind, Frank was a good cop. *Was* not as in is, but was as in before.

And though he believed Frank could still get the job done, he doubted the detective's ability to see the bigger picture. "How many tapes did you find?"

"Just this one," Frank lied. "I also saw a computer in the second apartment, but I didn't want to touch that until I talked to you first. There could be incriminating evidence against Donovan if the SOCO guys get their hands on the hard drive. Now if *you* want a warrant for the computer, you can make the necessary calls. But the bottom line is that this gives us motive for Donovan to be the shooter."

"Hold on, McKay. We aren't going to cut our own throats by pointing fingers at the Mayor's brother."

"I'm not suggesting we arrest him, Lieutenant. I'm saying we have a motive. Grayson used this tape to pressure Donovan into landing a couple of movie roles for the girl in this video. Grayson then threatened Donovan that he would go public with the tape if Donovan didn't do him another favor. Donovan clearly had the motive to benefit by Grayson's death."

"And you have a witness to these conversations between Grayson and Donovan?"

"Not one the lawyers wouldn't rip to shreds. It's just hearsay at this point."

"Do you know what this favor was?"

"Yeah, the girl in the video lived with Grayson, and then moved out on him. Grayson wanted Donovan's help in getting her back."

The Lieutenant rubbed his forehead with his fingers, being careful not to raise them higher into his perfectly sprayed hair. "Does Donovan have an alibi?"

"We didn't talk to him," Frank answered. "To be honest, I didn't think you'd want us ruffling his feathers."

"You'd love that, wouldn't you, McKay?"

"Of course. But not without with your permission."

Frank reached down, placing his fingers on the top of the tape. "Should I run this over to Sal Martin?"

"No," the Lieutenant answered sharply, pulling the tape towards him. "I'll call Donovan to let him know that you and Briggs are coming over. However, and you listen to me on this one, McKay…I don't want you mentioning or asking him any questions about this video tape. And whatever you *do* say, remember you are talking to the Mayor's brother."

"Yes sir," Frank complied. "You make the phone call and I'll get Lu."

Lula waited anxiously at her desk, watching the animation of the two men as they communicated behind the glass of the Lieutenant's office. "What was that all about?" she grilled Frank, continuing before he had time to answer. "You come in here, don't bother to say good morning or anything, and then walk by me as if I don't exist?" The irritation in Lula's voice was a splash of water over the anger that Frank had carried from the Lieutenant's office.

"I'm sorry, Lu," Frank apologized. "I had a lot on my mind. Are you ticked at me because I can't go to your niece's wedding?"

"No! I just want to know what you gave him."

Frank hunched over, laying his hands flat on Lula's desk. He spoke softly. "It's a tape of the Lieutenant's buddy Donovan with a very under-age Jennifer Goodman."

"Where did you get it?" questioned Lula in a low voice after a quick inspection of the activity of the other detectives in the room.

"Grayson had two apartments in his building. I found the tape in the second place."

"And that was all you found?"

"There was one more," Frank lied again. "That one had Jennifer rolling around with Harold Klinger, Grayson's former boss."

"Isn't Klinger the guy who killed himself?"

"Yeah."

"There's got to be more, isn't there?" Lula probed. "Wasn't there one of her with Doctor Epson?"

"Yeah, I guess you're right, Lu. Grayson must have more hiding somewhere," Frank answered slowly to recover from his mistake. "But for now, Tillman wants us to talk to Donovan and see if he has an alibi for the night of the murder."

"He does?"

"Yeah. He's calling Donovan now."

Lula stretched her neck, peeking around Frank and into the Lieutenant's office. As Tillman put down his phone, she rose from her chair. "Give me a minute, Frank. I need to talk to the Lieutenant alone."

Frank was now the outside observer as Lula entered the Lieutenant's office, closed the door, and began a muted dialogue, her arms alive with energy. The Lieutenant peered around her, into the squad room towards Frank, nodded his head with a positive signal, and Lula opened the door to the office and summoned Frank to join them.

"McKay," the Lieutenant began cautiously, "I changed my mind. I want Briggs, and only Briggs, to talk to Donovan. You go with her, but I don't want you in the same office with Donovan."

"Why?" challenged Frank, the word extending like a whole note responding to the press upon a piano key.

"Because this is a delicate matter and I don't want you upsetting Donovan with your smart-ass mouth."

Frank curled his fingers hard against his palms as he struggled to rein in his voice. But neither his face nor the darting glances of his eyes could hide his indignation at being outnumbered and maneuvered into a hopeless corner. He knew there was little chance that arguing further would reverse the change in the Lieutenant's decision.

"Okay, I'll just go along for the ride," he accepted. But he couldn't tame the passion of his spirit long enough to surrender without a final word. He pointed to the black plastic cassette, his eyes daring to push back at his superior once more. "That may be your ticket to making Captain, so don't forget who brought it to you."

"Get the hell out of here!" the Lieutenant scowled back, his cheeks and forehead blushing pink as he neared the limit of his impatience.

Frank waited until he and Lula were outside hearing distance of the Lieutenant's office before he released the words pushed through his clenched teeth. "Why did you do that?"

"Because, Frank," she answered with her face still locked in conflict. "I heard how you talked to that doctor and you can't expect to talk to a city official the same way. Face it, Frank, when it comes to your interview style you come up short of charm."

"And you think this idiot Donovan deserves to be treated like some kind of royalty?"

"There are times you have to tone down your style depending on who you are talking to. Donovan is the Mayor's brother, Frank. Yes, he *does* deserve to be treated differently."

For the first time since knowing her, Frank could feel the inner cracking as his anger was set alight by something Lula had said or done. And he realized as quickly that he was running short on people who weren't pushed at arms length outside his defensive walls.

"If you're going to be my partner, Lu," Frank whispered close to Lula's face. "You can't be stabbing me in the back like you just did."

"Don't give me that. I did what I just did because I *do* have your back," disputed Lula. "And if you're gonna be *my* partner, you've got to tell me everything. Sal Martin called me this morning. He told me I should keep my eyes open because of some ex-con named Luis Vega. Sal thought you would have said something to me about this guy, but you haven't. Why's that, Frank?"

Lula stormed off ahead of Frank, down the stairwell and onto the stairs leading from the precinct house. He pursued her, calling her name repeatedly. But she wouldn't slow her furious pace ahead of him until he finally caught up with her, grasping the side of her upper arm.

"Will you please stop and listen to me!" Frank pleaded. "I'm sorry, Lu. I should have talked to you before I went into Tillman's office. I'm sorry."

"Would you have done that if Corelli was still your partner?" she asked as she stopped her movement, pushing his hand from her arm.

"No," Frank lied, believing that Vince would never have gone behind his back as Lula had done.

And he was trying to defuse their argument, not feed it, so he had to keep his thoughts as thoughts. He had to lie.

"And what about this Vega?" demanded Lula. "Sal told me this guy wants you dead. Don't you think I should know if there's some crazy con out there with a gun in his hand, just waiting to take a shot at you? When were you going to tell me...when he shot *me* because I just happened to be in the way?"

"I'm not worried about Vega, Lu. The parole board wouldn't have released him if they thought he was going to kill a cop to celebrate his freedom."

"So what happened between you two?"

Frank forced a long, deep breath between his lips. "Sal and his partner at the time were serving an arrest warrant on Vega on a tip about a gang shooting. Stan Burdette and I went in as back up. Anyway, Sal was putting his cuffs on Vega in the stairwell outside the creep's apartment when Vega's little brother popped out of the door and began shooting. He hit Sal in the leg twice with the four shots he got off. I was in the clear, returned fire, and the kid was killed. It all happened so fast that I didn't realize until later that he was only thirteen."

"Firing that weapon made him a man," Lu replied instinctively.

Frank glanced into her glistening dark eyes, immune to the worn response he had heard too many times before. "Well, it turned out that Luis Vega had no involvement in the gang shooting for which we were arresting him, so his kid brother got killed over nothing. Vega made me the focus for his bitterness and vowed to kill me."

"Why was he in prison?"

"I didn't say Vega was a saint."

Frank waited outside Chicago's City Hall, observing the people going in and searching for Lula among those coming out. His eyes quickly lost interest with each figure in a suit, locking upon those whose slender legs darted down from a skirt or occasional dress. Until one uniformed police officer caught his attention. The officer followed his nurtured paunch through the tall doors, moved to the side, lit a cigarette, and after releasing a cloud of smoke upward, surveyed the faces around him until like Frank, he recognized a face.

As he approached Frank he secured the cigarette between his lips, freeing his hand to reach out towards Frank, the little white stick waving up and down as the words danced from his mouth. "Frankie McKay, how ya doing?"

"Neal Delaney," Frank greeted back, nodding towards the officer's uniform. "I thought you'd be out of that by now."

"Not me. After I failed my exam the third time, I figured I wasn't gonna try again. Besides, after four years in the military police and fifteen being a cop, I don't feel right *not* wearing a uniform."

"Do you sleep in that thing?"

"Sometimes I do, sometimes I do," Delaney answered. "Hey, I read about Corelli in the newspapers. I was sorry to hear about that, Frankie. He's a good guy. He hasn't deserved that bad run of luck he's had."

"I know."

"So how's everything going in homicide?"

"Same-o, Same-o," Frank answered. "It's not as fresh as it used to be. What about you?"

"I've got this cushy assignment," Delaney answered, his thumb pointing over his shoulder to City Hall. "It doesn't get any better than this, Frankie. They asked me if I wanted to be lead man on this detail, but I told my boss that I didn't want it. I'm happy doing what I'm doing at the level I'm at. What are you doing out here?"

"Waiting for my partner."

"Oh yeah? You do they have you paired with now?"

"Lula Briggs."

"Oh yeah, Briggs," acknowledged Delaney with a nod of his head. "I see her quite a bit in here."

"You do?"

"Sure, she's tight with the Mayor's brother. Not sexually or anything, but I see them talking to each other all the time."

Delaney looked down at his watch and the remaining length of his cigarette. "I need to get back inside, Frankie. It was real good seeing you again."

"Yeah," Frank replied.

Lula had lied to him about knowing Donovan. He wondered if she was the source who tipped off Donovan to Grayson's murder. At least it explained why she wanted to talk to Donovan alone, leaving Frank waiting as he did now, pacing anxiously for her reappearance.

Frank repeatedly looked down at his watch trying to push time forward with each glance. Not soon enough, Lula emerged from the building, her wide eyes downward, her lips pressed together.

"It didn't go well?" Frank asked.

"He's not our guy," Lula answered, looking past Frank. "He said he was at a business meeting.

I confirmed it with a few calls while I was still in there."

"You look upset, Lu."

"I'm just getting a headache. It was stuffy in there."

"Donovan didn't mind talking to you, even though he didn't know you?"

"He was cooperative and pleasant," she answered. "It helped that the Lieutenant had called to make the introduction and appointment. I want to see that second apartment, Frank."

"Why?"

"Because, we are in this case together. Now you can either take me there or I can go myself, but either way, I'm going."

The two detectives spoke very little on the way to the Grayson crime scene. As Frank focused on the city traffic, Lula looked away from him, staring out the side window, only a fraction of her face visible to his view of her. He followed the silhouette of her body, out and under the outward curve of her breasts and down to her fingers tapping nervously just above her knee.

"Where did you go after we had dinner the other night?" asked Frank, breaking a silence of voices.

"Home," she answered without turning to look at him.

"Do you know what happened to Paul Abbott that night?"

Frank waited for an answer while watching the cars ahead of him come to a stop at a red traffic signal. "Did you hear me, Lu?"

"No, I was thinking."

"I asked if you knew that Paul Abbott was

beaten and robbed the night we had dinner."

"Who?" she asked softly, the reflection of her eyes looking back at her from the side window.

"C'mon, Lu, Paul Abbott was the guy we talked to over at Crosswhite Investments."

"No," she answered. "I didn't hear about it."

Frank waited again, listening for the response that didn't come. He was curiously surprised at her indifference to his comments about Abbott. She didn't ask what happened, how he was, or what was stolen.

Lula broke her muted mood when they parked the car in front of a building a few doors from the crime scene address. "I'm going to leave my purse in the car, Frank. Be sure to lock the doors."

Frank led her through Grayson's second apartment, showing her the cable feed in the room above Jennifer Goodman's room one floor below. He led her into the office room in which he found the tapes and he watched as Lula searched the same closets and drawers and cabinets through which he had rummaged on his previous exploration. He stood in the hallway between the bedrooms, listening to his partner's movements while his thoughts simmered in the wait. This wasn't sitting right with him. Vince never second-guessed or doubted Frank's word. But then again, he left it open for Lula's mind that there *could* be more video tapes; and there were, but they were tucked away in Frank's apartment.

Lula poked her head out of the office where the tapes had been found. "Frank, did you do anything with the computer?

"No, isn't it still there?"

"It's still here. I meant did you try to turn it on and look at the contents."

"I hate computers, Lu," Frank answered. "I figured Sal Martin's crew would look it over." He followed her back into the room, surveying the sleeping computer and monitor.

Lula held her head, her eyelids cringing down over her eyes. "This headache is getting much worst, Frank. Do you think you can go back to the car and bring up my purse? I think I have some aspirin I can take."

"Sure," Frank answered, relieved at the opportunity to break up the boredom of standing around while he waited for his partner to finish her examination.

When he returned to the apartment, Lula told him that she was ready to leave. She fumbled through her purse, pulled out a little green bottle and headed to the kitchen for a glass of water. Frank glanced at the computer and noticed a light flashing beneath the monitor screen and a latex glove on the carpeting a few feet away. "Did you try to use the computer, Lu?"

She forced a little smile on her lips as she reappeared, though she still avoided looking at Frank's eyes. "Umm...just for a second. I only turned it on, then off again. Let's get out of here, Frank."

"Don't forget the glove you dropped on the floor," he answered, looking into the dark of her eyes.

Chapter Nineteen

The sight of Sal Martin and Ted Schwack sitting in the Lieutenant's office surprised both Frank and Lula when they returned to the precinct house. Frank quickly discarded Lula's opinion that they should wait for an invitation to join the meeting and hurried ahead of her through the open doorway.

"What's going on?" Frank asked.

"Martin and Schwack are going over to your victim's building to pick up that computer you found in the second apartment."

"You got a warrant?" questioned Frank, nodding at the official looking paper in Sal Martin's hand.

"You didn't think that I would, McKay?" the Lieutenant answered.

The other detectives looked up expecting a response from the detective they both knew well, but Frank defied their anticipation, remaining quiet.

"Coomer is meeting us there to lift prints," Sal spoke up. "Maybe some trace of this mystery man Nordhagen will pop up again in our sweep of this second location, Frank. We were just telling the Lieutenant that we contacted the Minneapolis police and found out Nordhagen had a missing daughter at the time he went to prison."

"Missing as in being abducted or as in running away?" Frank asked.

"Running away," Sal answered. "The Minneapolis PD had questioned him to rule out foul play, but Nordhagen's wife corroborated his story about the girl leaving on her own."

"This daughter was never found?" asked Frank.

Sal threw his arms up. "We don't know, Frank. The detective we talked to told us Nordhagen's wife took their other two kids and moved away. His guess was that they left the state. His theory is that Nordhagen's wife followed the missing daughter."

"Well, if this daughter went missing before he went to prison, then this wasn't something that happened in the last year, was it?"

"No, Frank," Sal answered. "This is going back five or six years."

"Did they have pictures of this missing daughter?"

"Not yet. Just a name...Berta."

"We have distributed pictures of Gunnar Nordhagen throughout the agencies in the city and suburbs, including the State police," Schwack told Frank, handing him a copy of Nordhagen's image. "If he's still in Illinois, we'll find him."

"Did your search turn up any more video tapes?" Lula asked the two SOCO officers.

"More?" responded Sal with a surprised look. "Not in the apartment in which Grayson was killed. We'll check out the second apartment when we get there."

"All of you keep talking about video tapes," the Lieutenant began. "But isn't it possible that he switched over to CDs or DVDs?"

"Your victim was fifty-five, Lieutenant," Schwack answered his question. "Based on what we found on his first computer, your victim hadn't kept up with technology."

"We'll know more when we check out this second apartment, Lieutenant," Sal answered. "I guess I'm a little lost on all this talk about video tapes and the victim's computers. Isn't our main push on this case to find evidence that will point to Grayson's killer?"

"McKay, you want to answer Sal's question?" the Lieutenant asked.

"Sure...we think there is a possibility that Grayson was blackmailing men after filming them having sex with an underage girl. It could be that our killer was one of those men. I was hoping the computer would turn up a list of names and addresses. We never found an address book at the first apartment."

"How does this guy Nordhagen fit into all of this?" Sal asked Frank.

"I think he's looking for his daughter."

"Sal," the Lieutenant spoke up from his chair, "Why don't you and Schwack head over to the crime scene. We need to put a priority on sweeping that place for evidence. I need to talk to McKay and Briggs privately."

The Lieutenant stood and closed the door behind the two departing officers from the SOCO team. He stepped slowly around Frank and Lula, stopping in front of Frank, the faces of the two men within the scent of each other's breath. "You'd better not be holding anything back from me, McKay. Are you sure there was only one tape?"

"That's what I gave you, wasn't it?"

The Lieutenant turned his interrogating view to Lula, who spoke up to the question in his eyes. "I only know about that tape Frank gave you this morning."

"Did Donovan have an alibi, Briggs?"

"Yes sir. It checked out."

"So, we can rule him out as the shooter?"

"Yes sir," Lula answered.

The Lieutenant resumed his slow steps, lifting his hand just above his hair before landing it upon the back of his neck. He turned to both detectives, filtering his thoughts into the selected words he was careful to share.

"As far as I'm concerned this tape of Donovan and this girl does not exist...*if* he has nothing to do with Grayson's murder. Am I clear on that, detectives?"

"Yes sir," Lula responded, drawing Frank's eyes towards her.

"What about you, McKay?" challenged the Lieutenant.

Frank paused for a moment before falling in line, "I'm just here to solve a homicide, Lieutenant."

Chapter Twenty

There were two voice messages waiting on Frank's desk phone—one from his brother Mickey and the other from Jennifer Goodman. He wanted to speak with Jennifer again, but he balked at the thought of returning Mickey's call. His brother only called when his need of money was the subject. Frank knew it was partially his own fault because he never turned off the faucet of cash flowing from his hands into his brother's pocket. After Mickey's second tour of living on the streets, Frank took his brother in for a few months. That experiment quickly wore thin with Frank's nagging intolerance of the younger McKay's binge drinking and heavy chain smoking. So Frank found a cheap apartment in the old neighborhood in the very same building in which they lived as kids, paid for the rent, and continued to subsidize his brother's welfare income. The cell phone he bought his brother was at first intended as a way for Frank to keep tabs on Mickey's whereabouts, but it soon became a lifeline between the needy and the burdened.

Frank returned Jennifer's call before he responded to his brother's message. Jennifer expressed her desire to talk to Frank alone, but not at Leo Salerno's place and not at the precinct house; and preferably after her six o'clock singing lesson.

So they agreed to meet at eight that night at the little outdoor café on the northern fringe of Buckingham Fountain in Chicago's Grant Park.

Mickey's response to Frank's return call was more urgent. He needed five hundred dollars and he needed it quickly, but would not give Frank a reason while on the phone. He pleaded with his big brother to meet him in one of the neighborhood bars just a few blocks from the location of Mickey's apartment.

Frank found Mickey sitting in a booth, in front of a half-filled glass, an empty bottle of beer, and an ashtray overflowing with the filter ends of spent cigarettes. Frank slid next to the table across from his brother, the long crevices tearing through the cushion beneath him drawing his glance as his hands ran across their ragged edges.

"So what's the big *emergency*, Mickey?" Frank queried.

"Did you bring five hundred bucks?"

"I just gave you forty the other day, Mick! Every time I turn around, you're asking for more. Now you call me and ask for five hundred. Not ten, not twenty, but five hundred. What happened to your welfare money?"

Mickey nervously tapped the sides of his head with the palms of his hands. "I lost most of it on the horses."

"What happened to your promise?"

"I know...I know...but I had this sure thing, Frank."

"And this sure thing didn't come through for you, right?" Frank didn't wait for his brother to answer. "No, they never come through for you. And who the hell ends up paying for your mistakes? C'mon Mick, who?"

"*You* do, Frank."

"Yeah, I do." Frank put his own hand over his mouth as if the gesture would hold back the escape of more words. But he had scolded his brother enough. "Why do you need five hundred?"

Mickey leaned forward and rolled his eyes to the right with an accompanied gentle tilt of his head. "See those two guys at the pool table? That big guy kind of...hustled me."

"Jeez, Mickey!"

"I thought I was better than him...really, Frank," claimed Mickey. "Then when I thought I was going to walk out of here with a wad of cash, he talked me into one more game for double or nothing...and I lost. Then I talked him into another game and I lost again. Now he won't let me leave here until I pay what I owe."

"You're *not* that good, Mickey," Frank declared. "You should have known you were being hustled."

Mickey looked back towards the pool table. "Crap! He's coming over here."

A heavy set, multi-tattooed man in curly black hair stepped next to the table where Frank and Mickey were seated. He stopped at the edge of the rectangle table, leaning forward on a pool stick held to his chest, creating an image resembling a towering tripod. "Does this *suit* have my money, Mickey?" the man asked in a deep tone, the venom in his voice referring to the well-dressed Frank.

"No," Frank quickly answered. "This suit doesn't have anything that belongs to you, bird brain."

The man scowled down at Frank, his eyebrows lowered. "What did you call me?"

"Bird," Frank repeated slowly, "...brain."

The big man hunched down towards Frank. "You think because you're wearing a suit that it makes you a bigger man than me?"

"No," Frank answered coolly, "I think because I'm carrying a badge and I can tell your parole officer that you're hustling a cop's brother...and we both know what that would mean to you...*that* makes me a big man."

"Let me see!" the man commanded, referring to the unseen badge. Frank exposed the butt of his holstered gun as he opened his jacket to reach for his shield, lifting the identification from his belt and up to the man's face.

The tattooed man glanced back and forth to both Frank and Mickey several times as he straightened his posture. "How about if I just forget the three hundred bucks and we'll just call this a little misunderstanding?"

"And in addition to forgetting this *three* hundred," Frank looked the man in the eyes before turning his stare to Mickey. "Mickey here, will apologize to you, and you won't try to take it out on him when I've got my back turned."

"Sure, man."

"Mickey?" Frank pushed the word across the dirty table top.

"I'm sorry," Mickey reluctantly muttered.

Frank stood as the man with the pool stick retreated, and motioned his brother to follow him out of the tavern.

"How did you know he was on parole?" Mickey inquired excitedly as the door behind them closed and their feet were on the sidewalk.

"Just a lucky guess."

"A guess?" Mickey asked astonished. "What if he would have said he *wasn't* on parole?"

Frank turned to his brother. "That was the first thing that came to my mind. I don't know what I would have done if he called my bluff. More importantly, why did you tell me you owed *five* hundred?"

"I'm sorry, Frank," defended Mickey as Frank turned away in a quickened pace. "You know me...I figured if I had a little extra I wouldn't have to ask you for more so soon again. I don't like asking you for money."

"You ask me for money all the time, Mickey!" Frank argued back, stopping his brisk walk to face his brother again. "I hate it when you lie to me! You were all ticked off and upset the other day when I told you I was changing my life insurance. You felt that I didn't trust you. But why should I when you lie to me like this?"

Mickey's eyes pointed downward to the pavement. "I'm trying to change, Frank," he uttered in a low voice.

Frank resumed his brisk pace, stopping at a bench just inside a small nearby park. He turned back to face Mickey before sitting down without voicing his intentions, his eyes surveying the idle, rust-spotted park equipment. Mickey followed his brother, covering a fraction of the initials carved into the wooden slats of the bench as he also sat, leaving a foot or more between the two men. His fingers searched through a package before he rolled and threw the ball of empty paper on the ground after the last cigarette was safely between his lips.

"You're littering," Frank complained.

"Like it really matters around here," Mickey muttered sarcastically.

The two brothers were quiet for a few minutes as each thought about the memories the old park was whispering back at them. "You know, Frank... one of my earliest memories is of Ma bringing us to this park. I used to love playing in that sand box over there, though it looks so much smaller now."

"Yeah, well...you've grown a little since then."

Mickey laughed, a short, muffled laugh lost quickly to a deep cough.

"Do you think any of our toy soldiers are still buried in there?" Mickey asked upon recovering his breath.

Frank shook his head. "No...but go check it out if you want. I'll wait here and keep an eye on you."

Mickey's eyes inspected the air above the park after Frank's response brought a smile to his face. "You know what I miss about Ma? The corned beef and cabbage she used to make. I remember having it every Saint Patrick's day, and on our birthdays, too. She had a way of cooking it all so tender that we only needed the sides of our forks to cut the beef and boiled spuds and cabbage. I can still feel that corned beef melting like cotton candy in my mouth. I miss that."

"That's funny," Frank replied. "Any time I've seen or heard about corned beef and cabbage, I think about your tenth birthday when the old man came home drunk and yelled at Ma about spending his beer money on your dinner and cake."

"Oh, yeah," Mickey remembered. "He threw his piece of cake at the fridge and it splattered all over the place. Then he chased me into our room after I yelled at the top of my lungs that I hated him...and then you came in to pull him off of me...and he beat the crap out of *you*."

Mickey glanced briefly at Frank before turning his view towards the sand box again. "I guess you're still running in to help me, Frank."

Frank remained silent as his thoughts recalled the beating. It was just one of a forgotten number of times that his father mistook him for a punching bag, whether it was in his effort to protect Mickey, his mother, or just himself.

"You know, Mickey," Frank said softly. "No matter how bad that all seems now, Ma somehow found a way to make us forget. She cooked every day of her married life, and no matter what she put on the table, it was always good and we always had three meals a day. She went to the Laundromat twice a week and our dresser drawers were always filled with clean socks and underwear. And I don't ever recall a time when she complained about not having a house of her own. And you know what else, Mick? I can't remember a time when I thanked her for everything she did for us. I don't remember ever hearing those words from you or the old man, either."

Mickey flicked the remainder of his cigarette into the sparse grass in front of them. "Do you ever wonder why she did it, Frank?"

Frank's eyes slowly watered as the memory pushed back into his mind. "As long as we live, we'll never know for sure. When I used to try not think about it, I figured that Ma had a reason to put up with the old man's crap when you and I were kids. But when we moved out...I don't know, Mick...I guess she had no more reason to endure it all." He paused a few moments before going on. "You and I were lucky in a way in that we never saw Ma the way the police found her. But about a year and a half after she passed, I got a call to a house in which a woman had hanged herself in her basement. She was younger than Ma was, but I saw Ma's features in her face. Of all the dead bodies I've seen, that one has remained the clearest in my memory."

"I've often wondered what she was thinking at the very end...and when I tried it, I just couldn't do it."

"What do you mean, Mickey? You tried to kill yourself?"

"Don't worry, Frank. I couldn't do it. I looked down the barrel of the gun with my finger on the trigger, and I thought and thought about it, but I couldn't do it."

"I don't believe what I'm hearing! Where did you get a gun?"

"It's just a little one that I bought off a guy in a bar."

"You don't need a gun, Mickey!" Frank refuted angrily. "And it doesn't matter if it's a *little* gun or a big gun...either way the bullets can kill you!"

"It's a tough neighborhood, Frank. I don't want anyone breaking in and stealing my stuff."

"What stuff? Everything you have in there is junk we bought at thrift stores or out of someone's yard. Get rid of the gun, Mick. Next time I come over, give it to me. I just can't believe the crazy things you do sometimes!"

Frank looked down at his watch. "I've got to get over to Grant Park. I'm meeting someone to talk over a case."

"Is it interesting?" Mickey asked.

"Is *what* interesting?"

"The case."

Frank looked down at his brother. "No. It's like any other case. We'll either figure things out or it'll go cold...and there will be another one right behind it."

"Frank?"

"What?"

"I'm out of smokes. Can you please lend me a twenty? That's all, just a twenty. I'll pay you back."

Frank reached into his pocket and withdrew a small fold of ten fifty dollar bills and handed four to his brother.

"I might be coming into some extra cash pretty soon. If I do, I promise I'll take care of you. But for now, you've got to ease up on this gimme, gimme all the time."

Frank turned to his brother one more time after walking a few feet away. "And keep your hands off that gun until I come over to get it."

Chapter Twenty-one

The tightening in Frank's chest that remained from his time with Mickey was soothed by the breeze blowing in across the surface of Lake Michigan and by the choreographed lines and arcs of water rising from Buckingham Fountain. In an hour or so, when the air darkened with the dipping of the sun behind the lakefront skyline, the fountain's light show would illuminate the dancing waters. In the meantime, Frank enjoyed the easy wait while his eyes scanned the fascinating variety of faces and bodies of the many figures moving between his spot at the small table and the edge of the jewel of Grant Park. His ears picked up the words of people talking at the tables behind him, and the sum of all the sights and sounds gave life to fresh thoughts, pushing those of his brother aside.

His body had already slipped unnoticed into a quiet calm when Jennifer glided into his view from the far edge of the fountain's wide circle. As if those around her were suddenly doused in unassuming whites and grays, her presence was brightly highlighted by her short dress the color of ripe sour cherries. She moved towards his table with the same motion as a nearby balloon connected by a string to a passing child's hand. Frank stood as his eyes slid slowly from the bottom limits of her dress and down her sleek legs to the small straps holding her high heels upon her open feet. Then up again his view rose, upward over her plunging neckline until his line of sight rested upon her young face.

"Have you been waiting a long time, Detective?" she asked as she sat in the open chair across from Frank, placing her small purse on the top of the round table.

"Not really," Frank answered as he returned to his sitting position. "Would you like something to drink?"

She turned and tilted her head sideways and brought her arms inward forming a V of bare skin from her neck down to the indentation between her breasts. "Let me think," she said coyly. "I think I'll have a white wine."

"Are you sure you're old enough?"

"Yes, do you need to see my ID?"

Frank motioned to the waitress working his section of tables and ordered a glass of wine and a refill on his coffee.

"You don't drink, Detective? You're not on duty, are you?"

"I don't have the same drinking gene as my father and brother. But I drink when I want to drink, and this is not one of those times. And no, I'm not on the clock."

"Does that mean I can call you by your first name...if you have one?"

"It's Frank."

Frank slipped quick glances at Jennifer's lips and eyes when her's were not aimed at him. Her glistening lip gloss reminded him of the outer skin of ready tomatoes. Her eye color was not unlike that of the late sky between the puffs of white clouds floating slowly over the lake, except that her eyes drew back his repeated peeks. And the slanting beam of the falling sun reflected off the delicate orange tint in her light brown hair, a long strand of which hung behind and down from her ear.

"Why did you pick this place?" Jennifer asked just as her wine and Frank's coffee arrived at the table.

"Because I enjoy it here," Frank answered. "I come here often to people watch and listen to what people say."

"You *listen* to people's conversations? Isn't that rude?"

"No," Frank shook his head, his eyes in direct contact with Jennifer's. "If you think about all the billions of people who have lived over the long stretch of history, you realize in listening that every combination of words has been used in the same sentences, using the same voice inflections and the same facial expressions. Every comment, every response, every line in a song, and every set of words in a book...they've all been done before."

"That sounds so sad and hopeless."

"The point, Jennifer, is that I've heard it all before. Take you for example. You probably had a rough childhood. You're either from a broken home or one of abuse. You ran away to the big city looking for something better, got hooked up with the wrong people, and now you find yourself in a situation from which you don't know how to escape."

As she listened to Frank's truthful words, Jennifer stroked the edge of her wine glass with one hand while her other hand rubbed the bottom of her exposed upper leg.

"Did Leo send you to talk to me?"

"No," she answered. "He told me that you found the video tapes. He doesn't know that I'm meeting you. I told him that I'm down here meeting a girlfriend."

"There was a young, blonde girl in one of the video tapes...it was her and Donovan. Tell me about her. I believe her name was Erin."

Jennifer hesitated as the one remaining doubt was squashed that Frank had indeed found the tapes. How would he otherwise know about Erin? "Damon brought her into the house last fall and hooked her up with Wade. She stayed in my room for a short time until last December...that's when Damon caught her using drugs and kicked her out."

"He kicked her out?"

"Yes," Jennifer answered. "Damon had no tolerance for drugs or smoking. He allowed wine as the only acceptable social drink. He told Erin to leave on one of the coldest nights of last winter."

"What was Erin's last name?"

"She said it was Smith, but I didn't believe her."

As he looked across the table, Frank sensed a fleeting aura of innocence in Jennifer's voice and in the indirect response of her eyes. "Why did you sleep with all those men, Jennifer?"

Jennifer placed an open hand over the visible crease between her breasts. "Because Damon asked me to. You can never understand. What my father took from me and gave me nothing in return, I gave for Damon and he gave me everything, more than I could ever dream of having back home."

"What was Leo's role in all of this?"

"He didn't approve. He wanted something more for me and something more for himself."

"And Wade Donovan?" Frank asked.

"Wade wants to send me away to Los Angeles. We got together the night that Damon was killed and Wade told me he would set me up with an apartment of my own and a bank account so that I can pursue a career in acting."

"I thought you were out with a girlfriend that night?"

"That's what I told Leo."

Frank thought about her answer before he remarked. "It sounds to me that Donovan wants you out of the picture because of his brother's run at the Governor's job. What does Leo think of Donovan's idea?"

"Oh, Leo doesn't know," Jennifer answered. "Leo wants me to pursue my dreams, but only if that means staying here in Chicago with him."

"And since you're being honest with me, what *are* your dreams, Jennifer? And why exactly did you want to meet me today?"

Jennifer leaned forward, dropping her hands around her glass, one holding the bottom, the other caressing the edge at the top. "For the first time in my life, I see a chance for me to change everything. For the first time in my life, I have found there is something about me in which I can believe. When Damon and Wade got me a part as an extra in my first movie, I knew *why* they did it. It wasn't purely for me. Then in the second movie I got to exchange a couple of lines of dialogue with a real movie star, and I loved it. And in the movie I just made, I had three lines of dialogue and the director and producer *both* told me that I had talent...and I didn't have to sleep with either one of them. Frank, this is *my* chance to change what I am."

"Then take it."

"I can't! Not as long as those tapes exist."

"So you *are* here on Leo's behalf, right?"

"No, Frank. Leo *wants* the tapes. I want them destroyed."

"So what is this, a bidding war between the two of you?"

Jennifer leaned back, tilting her head to open a clear path for her left hand to stroke downward from her ear to her shoulder while Frank's eyes followed on cue. "If you've seen those tapes, Frank—and I believe that you watched them closely—then you know what I can give you in return for destroying them."

Frank leaned forward, closing the gap between their faces. The young woman's eyes were again filled with self-assurance. "Jennifer, you are a beautiful woman in that sexy red dress cut just the right way. But there isn't anything on those tapes that is better than anything I've had before."

Jennifer's face slowly moved away from Frank's before she reeled back at the verbal sting of his next, unexpected question. "Did Gunnar Nordhagen kill Damon?"

Her mouth dropped open and her eyes widened as she grasped for an answer. But like a boxer shaking off the sweat to spy an opening for one more punch to his opponent, Frank continued his probe. "You know Gunnar Nordhagen...be honest with me!"

"He's my father," Jennifer answered faintly.

"And *your* real name is Berta Nordhagen."

"It's legally Jennifer Goodman," Jennifer answered slowly. "At least that is what Damon told me."

"We found your father's fingerprints in Damon's apartment. Did you know he was there?"

She shook her head, the emotions in her eyes continuing to change like the moving images in a turning kaleidoscope. "I didn't even know he was out of prison."

"And you haven't seen him here in Chicago?"

"No."

Frank studied Jennifer's face, again sensing the return of vulnerability exposed through her eyes. Suddenly across from him he saw the youth of his own two daughters and he pushed away from her to the back of his chair, his arms brought to rest upon his lap. He had put her through enough, for both of them.

"How about if I walk you to your car?" he suggested, ending their meeting as the lights in the fountain began to glow red on three tiers while the crown of spray atop blushed pink.

As they strolled slowly through the park on their way to the nearby parking garage, the other people-watchers took notice of them as well, though Frank was oblivious to being the subject of being watched. Whether it was the young woman in the red dress with her attractive long legs, or the contrast between the two of them together, the eyes of others were drawn to look at Frank and Jennifer.

"If my father is here," Jennifer asked as they walked. "How did he find me?"

"Did your mother know your new name and address?"

"No," denied Jennifer. "I haven't seen my mother since I left home. I sent her a couple of letters that she never responded to...and then they started coming back as addressee unknown."

"Don't you have other family?"

"Just on my father's side, but I don't care if I ever see any of them again. Do you have children, Frank?"

"Two daughters."

"Are you a good father to them?"

"Being a father isn't all that important," he answered.

"What do you mean?"

Frank had never shared his bitterness on the subject before, but it suddenly found a way out of him. "I always thought I was a good father when my girls were little. I cherished my time with them more than just about anything else. I always wanted to be to my daughters what my father wasn't to me and my brother. When they were little, I read to them, played with them, and took them to the park. One of my favorite things was pushing them both on the swings. I didn't like when they got hurt, from falls and things like that, but I loved it when they came to me for comfort. Then my wife handed me the divorce papers and when I read that I was allowed to see my girls every other weekend from six o'clock on Friday evening to six o'clock on Sunday, I realized how unimportant I was. I was no different than the dirt bags that I sent to prison, though *they* could see their families more frequently. I guess the only difference between me and them was that the guys in prison were on the inside looking out, while when it came to my girls, I was left on the outside looking in."

"I often prayed that my parents would get divorced," Jennifer replied. "It was miserable living with them."

"Sounds like my childhood," Frank confided.

Frank was at conflict with his own thoughts as they neared the entrance to the parking garage. What was right and wrong and what mattered and didn't matter had all become a jumbled mess over the past few days. And now he was confused about the young woman who walked beside him on the city streets. He had formed a disapproving opinion of the Jennifer seen in the video tapes, and the girl who lived with Damon Grayson and Leo Salerno. But now, as he glanced persistently at her young features in search of a read of what was going through her mind, his fatherly instincts wrestled for control against the logic of his cop intellect.

Frank noticed a comfortable smile on her face. "What are you smiling about?"

"I was just thinking about this feeling I have," she answered. "I usually put so much energy into wondering what a man wants from me that I don't remember feeling this safe before. I feel at ease walking next to you."

As she searched her purse for the keys to her car, Frank knew his time was running out to say something that would quiet the contradicting voices within him.

"Jennifer," he said as he stopped her with a gentle hand upon her arm. "I can't promise anything. But if these video tapes have nothing to do with Damon's murder...there's a chance they will never be needed to be seen by anyone."

Jennifer raised herself on the edges of her toes,

pressing her lips gently on the side of Frank's face. "Thank you."

The brush of human touch against his skin startled the hunger in Frank's loneliness, reawakening the conflict as he again glimpsed the woman in the girl before him.

"Frank!" a woman's voice echoed off the walls of the underground parking garage. It was Angie, moving briskly towards Frank and Jennifer. "So *this* is the reason you don't want me anymore!" Angie declared angrily while examining Jennifer quickly from the younger woman's face to her exposed cleavage.

"I didn't know you were married," Jennifer turned to Frank after spying the rings on Angie's hand.

"I'm not!"

"I can find my car from here, Frank," Jennifer announced as she scurried away, leaving an agitated Angie pulling on Frank's arm.

"No wonder you don't want me!" Angie cried. "How can I compete with that at my age?" Frank turned away uneasily as he noticed a few passersby looking in Angie's direction. Angie pulled open a light windbreaker and yanked the top of her blouse with both hands, sending two buttons through the air. "Here, how's this, Frank. Do I look like her now?"

Frank grasped his hands on Angie's arms. "Knock it off! You're making a scene! That girl is part of a murder investigation."

"Oh sure, Frank," Angie responded. "Do all of your murder suspects kiss you?"

"Damn it, Angie! It's not what you think it is."

Frank released her, did a half-turn, then turned

back to her again. "Why are you following me?"

"I don't understand why you don't want me anymore, Frank," she began to cry. "I saw you sitting alone by the fountain and I was going to surprise you when I saw her walk up to your table.

"Don't do this, Ange."

"I don't understand, Frank. I love you. Please, I can't go on like this without you. Why won't you love me back?"

"Angie...," Frank began as the first of four or five pops echoed off the walls from the next section of the garage. Frank turned his head in the direction of the sound.

"Go home!" he ordered Angie as he pulled the gun from his holster and sprinted in the direction of the gunshots. He screamed out his identity to several people fleeing away from the commotion, shouting "Which way?" to several until they pointed him to a car with an open door. Outside the car stood a short, stocky man hunched over the open driver's door, looking inside, his hand grasping a handgun pointed towards the pavement.

"Police! Put the gun down!" Frank shouted, his gun held firmly in both hands, aimed intently towards the man. "Put it down now and move away from the car!"

The burly man placed the gun on the concrete floor as he turned towards Frank with tears in his eyes. "My daughter...my daughter is shot."

"Move away from the car and get down on your knees," Frank ordered, pushing the man away with one hand as he continued to point his gun with the other. Frank glanced inside the car and recognized the red dress of the woman lying across the car seat.

"You stupid SOB!" Frank snarled the words at the man. Frank excitedly fumbled for the cell phone in the pocket of his jacket and got no further than flipping the cover open when a squad car squealed around a concrete pillar and came to a sliding stop not far from Frank. The reflection of its flashing blue lights bounced along the length of the garage walls.

"I'm a cop!" Frank yelled with his badge held up just as the two uniformed officers exited their car with their handguns drawn. "I need an ambulance!"

"You'll need two," the man kneeling on the ground spoke up. "I got the guy who shot my daughter. He's over there." He pointed past Frank's shoulder, towards the white and blue patrol car.

Frank turned towards the uniformed officers. "There's another shooter over there."

Both Frank and the man on the ground turned their heads to the car as they heard Jennifer moan, pleading faintly "Help me...please..." in between another moan that followed.

"Don't move!" Frank ordered the burly man before moving over to the passenger side of the car where he opened the door gently. Jennifer's right arm fell over the edge of the seat as Frank stooped over her. "It's Frank, Jennifer...there's an ambulance on the way...hang in there, kid." Frank pushed Jennifer slightly to find the source of the blood pool on the front seat below her, exposing a small hole in her upper left shoulder.

One of the uniformed officers rushed to the car. "I found the shooter. He's still alive...you wanna talk to him?"

"Yeah," Frank answered with anger in his

voice, telling the officer to stay with Jennifer.

"We've got two buses on the way," the officer standing guard over the downed shooter informed Frank.

The figure lying in a pool of blood on the hard floor between two cars was dressed in black shoes, black pants, black gloves, a bulky black vest, and a black ski mask and was writhing in pain. Frank pulled the ski mask up and back, exposing the milk chocolate skin of the shooter's neck, then chin, and then the mouth and eyes that Frank recognized.

"Lu!" Frank exclaimed. "Damn it, Lu!"

"I'm sorry Frank...I had to...Donovan wanted her dead."

Frank unzipped the down filled vest. As it oozed from the frayed edged hole in the middle of her exposed shirt, Lula's blood was as red as red is meant, but darkened as the black material absorbed it slowly into an expanding wet stain. Frank's hand turned scarlet as well as he placed it on her left arm where a second bullet had hit above her elbow.

"I can't...breathe...Frank," she stammered with fear in her eyes and voice.

"Hang it there, Lu. Please, hang in there."

"I'm sorry, Frank. Donovan is paying for Jamal's education...I had to do it."

"What about the Lieutenant?" Frank asked her, holding her hand as she squeezed tightly.

"He didn't do this...he only told Donovan...that he got rid of...the tape you gave him."

The first of the two ambulances screeched into the garage, stopping behind the squad car. "She goes first!" Frank ordered the uniformed officer, pointing to Lula as he stood. "I'm going to ride with her. No one talks to that other shooter until I do!"

"He's gone."

"What?"

"I don't know, he took off...but we got his weapon."

Frank rode in the back of the ambulance with Lula, staying with her until the emergency room doctor separated the grip of their hands. Unlike the red he washed off his fingers and palms before he called Jamal, his shirt and pants and jacket remained smeared in a mix of blood from both Lula and Jennifer.

Chapter Twenty-two

Frank lifted his badge as he passed the eyes of the uniformed officer standing outside the intensive care unit where Lula remained after a night of surgery. The translucent tube taped across her mouth underlined the fragility of her condition as a nearby ventilator swooshed in tandem with the up and down movement in the white sheet pulled up to her chest. A thinner line dropped down from a bag of clear liquid slowly sending drips of nourishment into her arm. Other lines and cables in white, red and black casings, led to the battery of monitors flashing and pulsating with a series of pings and mild white noise keeping vigil over the fallen officer. Like shades pulled down on a rainy day, her eyelids kept the outer world at bay as her weakened body struggled in silence to recover from the damage of the two bullets that had pierced through her skin. Frank's numbed hush crackled into mumbled profanities as his eyes seared upon the handcuffs linking Lula's still arm to the metal side rail of the bed. He pulled from his pocket the key of his own handcuffs, but it wouldn't unlock the pair preventing Lula's escape.

"What do you think you're doing, Frank?" the voice of Pete Richter startled Frank from behind.

"Get these off her!" Frank demanded.

"Sorry, Frank," Richter replied. "Your partner

is under arrest for attempted murder. The handcuffs are required per department regulations."

"I don't give a crap about regulations. It doesn't look like Lu is going anywhere in this condition."

"Maybe you *should* give a crap about department regulations, Frank," Richter responded as he stepped to the opposite side of Lula's bed, calmly glancing down at her face. "There is a pile of questions waiting to be answered, and you've got a lot of explaining to do. The circumstances of this shooting aren't looking good for *you* either, Frank."

"Well, that's where we differ, Pete. I don't make judgments based on circumstances."

"Maybe you'd like to explain why your partner knew where to find Jennifer Goodman? With you as close by as you were, it gives the appearance of being a set up."

"That's crazy! I don't know why Lu was there. I'm working on it."

"No, you're not, Frank," Richter replied. "The shooting in the garage is not your case. As a matter of fact, after I talk to Lieutenant Tillman, you won't be on *any* case until I get all the questions I have on this one answered."

Frank folded his arms with his fists closed tightly, lowering his eyebrows as he replied back. "You'd better be careful what you accuse me of, Pete. I might just shove it back down your throat."

"Don't bully me, Frank. Threats don't stop me. They never do," Richter replied, unaffected by Frank's words. "I already have a statement from Miss Goodman that you and her met on a date..."

"It wasn't a date!" Frank interrupted.

Richter held up his hand. "Hey, let me finish... she said the two of you met at Buckingham Fountain, a meeting place that *you* chose, not her. Are you denying her statement?"

"You've got it all wrong."

"Sure I do, Frank. Your Lieutenant knew nothing about your meeting with Miss Goodman. He confirmed that you were not on the job. And bottom line, you had no business being with a key subject in an ongoing investigation in the situation in which you were caught."

Frank didn't like what he was hearing from the Internal Affairs officer, but he understood how bad it was beginning to sound. "What's with you, Pete? Why are you crawling up my back?"

"*Because*," Richter answered back sharply, "You've always been one of the good guys, Frank. I hate this situation. The thought that you could be involved in all of this makes me sick."

Frank looked away with a momentary look at Lula's face before turning back to Richter with his voice lowered. "Why were you asking me about Lu the other day? Was she the focus of your investigation, or just a part of it?"

"I can't talk about that, Frank," Richter replied. "Unless you know some specifics that you'd like to share to save your own butt."

"And just how far up the ladder are you willing to go before you back down, Pete?"

"It depends."

"That answer isn't good enough for me." Frank said before turning for the doorway.

"I'll be seeing Tillman later, Frank. And then I'll be talking to you again."

Frank turned back to face Richter, throwing back his own bluff. "Go ahead, Pete. But the moment you talk to Tillman will be the moment you blow any chances of getting the person a step up from Lu."

As soon as Leo Salerno began to open his door, Frank kicked it wide open with the force of his foot, knocking Salerno to the floor. Frank closed the door behind him with his hands covered in latex gloves, turned the lock and knelt next to the cowering man.

"There isn't anything I hate more than being lied to, Leo. And right now, I have an advantage over you because I already know some of the answers to some of the questions I am about to ask. You can stand up now...slowly...and quietly"

Frank held his hand in front of Salerno. "The purpose of these gloves is so that I don't leave any fingerprints...not so much on your skin, but on this gun called a throw-away. Do you know what a throw-away is, Leo?"

Leo shook his head nervously as Frank pulled his service revolver from the holster beneath his jacket. "A throw-away is a gun that has no serial number and can't be traced back to me as the owner, legal or not. And if I should shoot your puny little brains out of your puny little head, no one could trace this nifty little murder weapon back to me. And because I am wearing these cool looking gloves, my fingerprints would be nowhere to be found."

"Are you going to kill me?"

"That's entirely up to you, Leo," Frank answered in a cool tone. "Now you might not be able to detect it in my voice, because I'm speaking softly and calmly, but I'm ticked off at you, Leo. Do you know why?"

"No," Salerno responded.

"No? That's the wrong answer, Leo. I know you knew the correct answer to that question," Frank raised his voice, pushing Salerno in the chest so that he fell into a sitting position on the couch. "I'll let you slide on that one...but only that one...okay?"

"Yes."

"Now, just so that we both understand each other, I'll remind you why I'm a little...no...make that *very* angry with you. You see, not only did your big mouth almost get Jennifer killed, but your big mouth almost got my partner killed. And now my partner is in very deep doo-doo. So you can see why I'd be furious, ready to lose my temper and beat you to a bloody pulp, right?"

"Yes," Salerno admitted. "I am so sorry about Jennifer. I never meant that to happen."

"You mean you're not sorry about my partner?"

"No...yes, I'm sorry about her, too."

"Okay, here's your big chance, Leo. Are you ready?" Frank asked, waiting for Salerno to nod nervously before he continued. "How did Wade Donovan know that Jennifer was going to be in Grant Park? And remember, I know some of the answers already."

"*I* told him. But I swear to you, Detective. I didn't know what was going to happen." Salerno held his abdomen and began to rock back and forth.

"What's the matter, Leo?"

"My stomach is starting to ache."

"Oh my, Leo. Are your nerves getting to you?"

"I didn't expect this to happen."

"Jeez, Leo. I don't understand. You don't actually know what happened at Grant Park, but you've put one and one together and figured out that it had something to do with Donovan. Hmmmm."

"Please, Detective," Salerno pleaded, his hands flattened together. "He was angry and worried that Jennifer would tell her story and ruin the Mayor's political career. I begged him not to hurt her, but he wouldn't listen to me. I begged him. I swear to you that I begged him not to hurt her."

"Well, whatever begging you did, it wasn't good enough. Was it, Leo?" Frank placed his gun inside his holster. "Tell me, Leo. Why do you want the video tapes of Jennifer?"

Salerno cautiously stood up from the couch, keeping his worried eyes on Frank's reaction. "Look at me. You've seen Jennifer. I have always been the *other* uncle in her life. Damon controlled her and I hated the things he made her do. I wanted her...I wanted her to love me. If I had the tapes, I could persuade her to stay. And if she stayed with me, I *know* she would learn to love me in the same way I love her. Without them, she will leave. Can you understand that, Detective?"

"No, Leo...I don't," Frank answered before he turned his back on Salerno and exited the apartment, leaving the man to wallow in his own self pity. Frank often wondered why his compassion excluded the rich, or those who he considered better off or in positions of power. Salerno obviously had money, and it didn't matter if it was honestly earned or not. Frank still thought of Salerno as a pathetic being, and in some small way that was enough to justify his own behavior.

Sal Martin was concentrating on reading lab results when Frank tapped him on the shoulder and sat in the open chair next to his desk.

"Hey, Frank," greeted Sal. "It's been a shock to all of us...you know, about Lula. How is she?"

"Not good. She's hanging on, but they're still listing her condition as critical."

Sal pushed a lab report towards Frank. "You must have a spy over at the lab, Frank. You showed up not long after I got this."

Frank dismissed Sal's comment as he looked down at the paper. "What's this?"

"The crew in ballistics worked all night on this one. The slug that hit Lula in the arm was a through and through and was compressed when it hit a concrete pillar. The one taken out of her chest matched the two taken out of Grayson's body. Ballistics also matched both sets to slugs test fired out of the Smith and Wesson Model Sixty that we found next to Jennifer Goodman's car. And the prints lifted off that gun matched those of Gunnar Nordhagen... so you've got a slam-dunk on both shootings."

"Yeah, I just don't have Nordhagen...and it looks like Internal Affairs will yank me off the case before I get him."

"Why?"

"Lu's my partner, Sal," Frank answered. "And it looks like what she did was tied to the Grayson case."

Sal didn't answer Frank; he understood the logic. He reached for a cream colored folder lying on the top of his desk. "I followed up on your phone message," he said as he opened the folder. "We got lucky in our first pass through the morgue records and matched that second set of female prints in Grayson's apartment to a Jane Doe who was found frozen to death last December."

"Really," Frank's curiosity was sparked. "Where was she found? How old was she?"

"She was found two blocks from Grayson's address, and the coroner estimated her age to be fourteen or fifteen...tops. Do you recognize the picture?" Sal flipped two photos of the dead girl onto his desk in front of Frank.

Frank scrutinized the facial pictures of the lighter than pale skinned girl, her eyes closed in peaceful sleep. Her blonde hair had fallen away to the silver surface beneath her, exposing the girl's softened features—features that appeared familiar to Frank's experienced eyes. He had seen her in the video tape with Wade Donovan. She was likely the same young girl who Frank only knew as Erin. But he wasn't certain. He would need to watch the video again and study her living and dead faces to convince himself that what he believed was true.

"Did they do any toxicology tests on her?"

Sal ran a finger over the print of the second page in the folder. "Yes, they found traces of cocaine and marijuana...oh! I didn't see this before...she was pregnant as well."

"Let me see that, Sal," requested Frank.

As Frank read over the report, Sal asked, "Do you have a name for this girl?"

"Erin...you can try Smith as a last name, but that's probably not it. Can you do a search for the name Erin through missing persons? I think this girl was a runaway."

"Sure. Do you think this is Nordhagen's missing daughter?"

"No, she's too young. I need to borrow this folder and show these photos to Jennifer Goodman, Sal," voiced Frank. "If this girl is who I think she is, Jennifer can confirm the ID."

Sal nodded. "By the way, our check of that second computer came up empty. It looks like someone went through it recently and deleted a huge chunk of files. We found nothing that links Nordhagen to Grayson in what was left, but we did find enough to figure out that your victim was no boy scout. He was into a lot of smut, but there doesn't seem to be anything tying him to specific names. Do you know if anyone else had access to that apartment?"

Frank thought back to his last visit to the crime scene with Lula, when he noted the light flashing on the monitor. "No," he answered. "I appreciate all the work every one has done on this, Sal. Tell them thanks for rushing the ballistics tests."

"I will, Frank," replied Sal. "But Pete Richter was the guy who lit the fire under the ballistics team."

"Richter?" Frank responded with surprise.

"Yes. Pete feels that he owes you, Frank. We both do. If you hadn't reacted as fast as you did when Vega's brother started shooting at us, there's a chance neither one of us would be alive today."

Frank pushed off the desk to a standing position next to Sal, placing his hand on the sitting officer's back. "Thanks, Sal."

Chapter Twenty-three

Frank listened to his thoughts and people-watched as he waited in the family room on the Intensive Care Unit, leaving once during each long passing hour to make the elevator trip up to the cafeteria and then down again with a fresh cup of coffee in hand. The skin on his fingers magnified the emerging coarse hairs as his hand rubbed over both sides of his tired face. When the flurry of visual activity marked the change of nursing shifts, Frank introduced himself to the oncoming staff and again requested that he be notified of any changes in Lula's condition. She had only briefly opened her eyes during the night. That fleeting movement however, was not enough to lift the guarded tone in the voices bringing that news to Frank.

The small morning window for visits by immediate family was less than sixty minutes away and Frank hoped to see Lula's mother and sister and Jamal. Surely they all had questions running close behind their worry, and Frank thought that his being there could ease their anguish. His cell phone vibrated as it had done repeatedly throughout the day and evening before and once again the incoming number was one identifying Lieutenant Tillman as the caller. Frank closed the cover and returned the phone to his pocket.

As the long hand on the family room clock climbed to the top of the circle, Jamal and his grandmother sauntered cautiously through the doorway. Frank stood to greet them, introducing himself as Lula's partner and telling them "...she's a strong woman. She'll make it through this."

After Lula's mother wiped away the tears that crept downward from her tired eyes, she looked up at Frank. "Lula talks about you all the time. My daughter thinks the world of you, young man."

There was a nostalgic sound to being called young man because rarely did anyone refer to Frank in that term any longer.

"Why are there handcuffs on my mother?" Jamal demanded with anger in his young voice. "The doctor said she was under arrest, but no one has explained any of this to us."

"No...don't listen to anyone who tells you she's under arrest. If she was arrested, she'd have charges filed against her."

"I *don't* understand this!" Lula's son argued. "Mom told Gram and me that she was going out for awhile. She never said anything about going to work."

Frank looked into the faces of both, their eyes pleading for an answer. Lula had shown Frank photographs of Jamal on several occasions, and in seeing him in person now, Frank noted his features, his hazel eyes. "I don't know," he lied. "It's a shooting between a police officer and a civilian and the cuffs are department rules. I don't like it, either. We're trying to put it all together. But right now the important thing is getting your mother well again."

"Would the handcuffs be on her if she was white?" Jamal challenged.

"Jamal, don't talk like that," his grandmother pulled on his arm.

"No, Gram!" he argued. "I'm asking *him* the question." Jamal stared at Frank, waiting for a reply.

"Like I said, Jamal. I'm trying to straighten this out."

After a short pause, Jamal asked. "Did you catch the person who shot her?"

Frank shook his head. "Not yet Jamal. We know who he is. We have his weapon and we'll get him soon enough. I promise."

"What color is he?" Jamal questioned, his brows lowered over the hostility in his voice.

Frank glanced to Lula's mother to include her in his answer to Jamal. "My color." Jamal turned his defiant look away from Frank, who turned to the young man's grandmother. "Can I talk to you alone for a moment?"

"Yes."

Frank led her gently by the arm, down the hall, far enough that Jamal could not overhear their voices.

"Tell me what you know about Wade Donovan," Frank said softly.

Lula's mother turned her eyes away from him without replying.

"I know that he's been paying for Jamal's schooling," stated Frank, trying to make contact with her eyes. "Lu didn't tell me why, but I think when I look at your grandson's face, the answer is there."

"You can't tell him!" Lula's mother pleaded.

"I won't do that."

Lula's mother glanced down the hall to her grandson before she went on. "My daughter was involved with Donovan when she met her first husband. Did you know her Clarence?"

"No, I never met him."

"He was a fine young man. I was so happy when Lula started bringing him around. I didn't like that Donovan...not because he was white, but because he didn't treat her right. She loved the man anyway, even though he was married. But he wouldn't leave his white wife to be with my daughter and she ended it between them."

"I didn't know that."

Lula's mother once again took a quick look down the hall at her grandson before she continued. "When Donovan found out that Lula and Clarence were going to get married, he started calling her again until she agreed to meet him once more before her wedding."

"And Jamal was his son?"

Lula's mother looked up at the ceiling, tears slowly rolling down the skin beneath her eyes. "Oh Lord, forgive me."

Frank reached forward, extending his hand with a gentle touch to the side of her arm. "It must have been hard for you to carry such a secret."

"Jamal doesn't know," she answered quietly. "Clarence never knew the truth. He loved that boy more than he loved life."

"Does Donovan know?"

"Yes. Lula told him a few years after she got rid of that poor excuse for a man who was her second husband. She wanted so much for her boy, and she was afraid she couldn't give him everything she wanted. So she went to Donovan."

"What did Donovan say to her?"

"I don't know. Lula only told me that she made sure that Jamal would get a good education. That's all she told me."

Lula's sister arrived soon and as Jamal, his aunt, and grandmother left the family room to resume their vigil in the ICU, Frank left the hospital and drove to the precinct house. He slowly typed his report of the shooting between repeated anxious looks up as he waited for the Lieutenant's arrival. Frank's eyes were focused on the printed version in his hands when the voice of the Lieutenant caused his hands to rattle the paper. "Where the hell have you been, McKay? I've been trying to call you."

"I've been at the hospital."

The Lieutenant looked down at Frank. "I don't want you to move an inch. Do you understand me? I'm going to check my messages, and then I want you in my office."

The Lieutenant stormed off through the doorway of his office as Frank watched him in muted anger, ignoring the inquisitive gaze of the other detectives in the room. His teeth clamped down on the inside of his lips as he spied upon the seemingly deliberate activity of the Lieutenant, who slowly hung his suit coat on a hook secured to the wall behind his desk. Frank continued to watch and wait as the Lieutenant picked up his phone once, placed it between his shoulder and ear and punched in the numbers of one call, his mouth moving and his face smiling. Then he repeated the same motions once again with his mouth moving, though the words were too distant for Frank's ears. And then once more while Frank's tolerance of the man continued to unravel like the fibers of a damaged rope, the Lieutenant's hand shook and his lips moved silently over the mouthpiece and once again his facial expressions locked into the serious configuration familiar to Frank. The Lieutenant looked out through the glass and gestured Frank to come forward.

Frank closed the door behind him and didn't wait for the Lieutenant to grant him permission to speak. "This is my report of what happened in the garage," Frank declared as he dropped the stapled sheets of paper on the top of the desk. "It's all there... including Lu's admission that you told Donovan that you destroyed the video tape I gave you."

The Lieutenant picked up the report, scanned it quickly, and then placed it in the top drawer of his desk. "Briggs is dead, McKay."

The unexpected words stunned Frank. "What? I just *came* from the hospital. She was alive."

"She died forty minutes ago. Nothing you claim to have heard from her can be corroborated."

"You can't do this!"

The Lieutenant pounded his fist on the top of his desk, rattling the contents of a cup filled with pens and pencils. "Don't tell me what I can or cannot do!"

"Did you destroy the tape or not?" Frank demanded.

"I have no idea what you're talking about, McKay. What tape?"

"You know damn well."

"No, I don't, McKay," the Lieutenant responded. "And do you really think anyone in their right mind is going to believe a dirty cop's reported confession over that of a decorated police Lieutenant and a respected member of the Mayor's office?"

"Briggs wasn't dirty!"

"Right, McKay! Briggs wasn't dirty and Corelli isn't crazy. Tell me, why is it that *your* partners are the rotten apples?"

"Don't you *dare* bring Vince into this. You should have had the balls to back him up, Barry. He was a good detective, much better than I ever was...and when he needed your help the most, you let him down."

"I'm not risking my career for any mistakes made by a failed cop. I will always have the back of any detective who does the job right. But don't expect me to cover the backs of those who screw up."

"Why not? You seem to have Donovan's back. Or don't your rules apply to those in high places?"

"Watch your mouth, McKay!" the Lieutenant stood up, pushing his chair against the back wall with a loud bang. "Get out of here."

"What about my report?"

"There is no report," the Lieutenant answered. "It's not your case. What happened with Briggs is an Internal Affairs investigation, and they will decide what went down after *they* talk to the witnesses and persons of interest, and that includes you."

"Fine, when do I talk to them?"

"Richter is waiting for you over at Headquarters."

Frank turned slowly to leave.

"And McKay," the Lieutenant called out. "You are off the Grayson case. I want all of your notes before you go over to IA. And one more thing...this alleged relationship between Donovan and I doesn't exist. If Internal Affairs was to get the wrong idea... Corelli just might find himself out of a job *and* a pension."

Chapter Twenty-four

Frank had been on the sweating end of the Internal Affairs interview table once before—when he shot Miguel Vega. His partner back then was the seasoned Stan Burdette who coached him to "stick to the truth and everything will be fine." This time however, the whirlpool of lies was stirred the moment Frank accepted his own decision to remove the video tapes from Damon Grayson's second apartment. And now he worried that anything he could say threatened to drag him deeper. But as various scenarios and attempts at logic tumbled through his thoughts as he waited in the pristine interrogation room, Frank could not commit himself to telling the truth.

Lula Briggs was dead. Frank could tell Pete Richter of Lu's last alert words spoken while she lay on the garage floor, words that implicated Wade Donovan and identified her as a corrupted cop. That could likely lead to a loss of survivor benefits for Jamal, who would also live his life with the shame of his mother's mistake. That would also end Donovan's financial support.

On the other hand, Frank could tell the story running through his head, putting a spin on some of the truth while denying the balance in an attempt to make it look like Lu was killed on the job. The flipside of that version would unjustly mark Gunnar

Nordhagen as a cop killer. There was no doubt in Frank's mind that Jennifer's father killed Grayson and a good lawyer could work the sentence down in the minds of a jury and judge by portraying the victim as a dirt bag. But there would be no chance of a lighter sentence if Nordhagen was convicted of killing a police officer. Perhaps Nordhagen deserved to be in prison either way, though Frank knew little of the man to substantiate that stretch of reasoning. But did he deserve to be a man in a prison cell or on death row for the rest of his life?

The humor of where he sat was not missed by Frank as he looked at the new carpeting and ran the palm of his hand over the shiny table top. Even the walls were without scuff marks, unlike those of the interview rooms back at the precinct. Back in his house, the carpeting was stained from spills of coffee and pop and unknown drops of body fluids. And the edges and the legs of the tables in his house were scratched and dented from the pounding of hands and the rubbing of the metal hand cuffs. And yet here, in a room clean enough to be mistaken as one in a doctor's office, Internal Affairs sought to identify the incompetent, if not dirtiest of cops.

Pete Richter put an end to Frank's struggle with the silence, stepping into the room with a cream colored folder in one hand and a small tape recorder in the other. "I'm sorry I kept you waiting, Frank," he said as he placed the contents from his hands one after one upon the table top before deliberately hanging his suit jacket over the back of the chair in which he sat slowly. Frank knew the routine of course; he and Vince had often pulled persons of interest into the interview room back at the house, leaving them there alone to stew in their thoughts until the detectives decided that the time to ask questions had come.

"I'm also sorry to hear about Briggs' death," Richter continued as he settled in his chair. "How long were the two of you partners?"

"Not long," Frank answered. "She was transferred into our squad probably three years ago…so we knew each other as co-workers. But Vince Corelli was my partner up until a couple of months ago. But you already knew all that, Pete."

Richter lifted a pair of reading glasses from his shirt pocket, adjusting the frame on his ears and nose with both hands with the speed of thick syrup. Such was his style, beginning slow and saving his acceleration of questions for later in the interview. He pushed a small black button on the tape recorder before peeking at Frank over the top of the wire-encased circles of glass on his face. "Before we get started I want to make it clear that you are not accused of any crimes, though you have the right to be represented by an attorney during this interview. Do you wish to postpone this interview until you have a lawyer present?"

"No, Pete," Frank replied. "I don't need an attorney. I understand my rights...and I'm fine talking to you."

"Okay…please state your full name," Richter asked as he opened the folder before him.

"Frank Walter McKay."

"And you are a detective 2nd grade…badge number five-two-seven-seven-eight?"

"Yes."

Richter moved the folder slightly to his right and slid a ruled pad of paper to his left. He reached into his pocket slowly, pulling out two pens, removing the cap of each before scribbling jagged lines on the uppermost margin of the top page of paper with both. "I think I'll use this one," he said as he slowly replaced the cap on the unworthy pen and slipped it slowly into his pocket.

"Do you want coffee or anything else before we get started, Frank?" Richter asked the question he always used at this part of his interrogation.

"No, let's get started," Frank answered impatiently while rubbing his palms together, his elbows resting on the table top. His irritation at Richter's method prompted him to add a few silent profanities as he looked at the double chin at the bottom of the interviewer's round face.

"Okay," acknowledged Richter. "How do you know Jennifer Goodman?"

"She was a person of interest in the murder case of Damon Grayson. She had lived with Grayson previous to the murder, and was among the people that Detective Briggs and I had interviewed...and sought to interview further."

"Did you ask Miss Goodman to meet you in Grant Park on the evening of May 9th on what she called a date?"

"Look at me, Pete," Frank answered. "I am old enough to be her father. Do you think a young woman like Jennifer Goodman would seriously want to date someone who looks like me? Use some common sense here."

"If it wasn't a date, why did you meet her there?"

"Because she wasn't available earlier in the day. She called and left me a message on my phone saying she would be available later in the evening, and thus we agreed to meet when we did at a very public place. Check her phone records...check mine."

"Then please explain why your Lieutenant was not aware of the meeting," challenged Richter. "You weren't on duty at the time, isn't that true?"

"No, that's not true. There are times when witnesses or subjects in a case are not available during my shift hours. This was one of those cases."

"But there are other detectives on other shifts."

"This was *my* case and I had *my* questions for Jennifer—Miss Goodman. I needed to hear her answers myself."

"*Your* case? Not yours and Briggs?" Richter quickly questioned back.

Frank glared back across the table. "Of course it was our case together. Why the hell do you think she was there?"

Frank's answer lifted Richter's eyes over the frames of his glasses once again while his heavy eyebrows lowered. "Are you now admitting that you knew Briggs was there?"

"Of course," Frank answered. "We were worried about Miss Goodman's safety. Lu was my backup."

"Wait a minute, Frank," Richter responded. "When we were at the hospital, you told me that you didn't know why Briggs was in the garage."

"I misunderstood you. I knew she was somewhere, keeping her distance, staying out of sight while she backed me up. But I didn't know why she was in *that* specific spot at *that* specific moment."

"You don't need to cover for her, Frank."

"I'm not."

Richter studied the facial expressions in Frank's answer that could not be recorded on the audio tape. "Why was Miss Goodman in danger?"

"Because…she is really Berta Nordhagen. Her father is Gunnar Nordhagen, our prime suspect in the Grayson murder…her father is also the man who shot Detective Briggs."

"And how do you know this?"

"The same goddamn way you should know… by reading Sal Martin's reports. Nordhagen's fingerprints were in Grayson's apartment. They're also on the weapon left at the scene. The bullets from that weapon were pulled out of the body of Grayson as well as from Briggs. We had reason to believe that he was also coming after his daughter. And jeez, Pete…it looks like we were right."

Richter quickly thumbed through the papers in his open folder. He ran the nails of his finger tips through his thin hair, bringing his right hand to rest under his cheek. "Then why was Briggs dressed as she was? I don't understand the ski mask. It just doesn't jive, Frank."

Frank shook his head and threw his arms outward. "I just don't know. I wanted to ask that question of Lu, but I never had the chance. I don't understand why she was wearing the mask. I don't understand why she was dressed like she was." Frank knew of course, he had put it all together that she was also the person who beat and robbed Paul Abbott. The down vest was most likely her attempt to conceal that she was a woman. And if that was indeed her intent, it seemed to have worked.

Richter carefully wrote out notes with his left hand, stopped, and lifted the pen to his mouth, tapping the non-writing end against his lips as if trying to gently awaken his next question. "If you were in the garage with Miss Goodman, then why didn't you walk her all the way to her car?"

Frank's mind raced for a moment. He didn't want to bring Angie's sudden appearance in the garage into his statement. If Richter knew about Angie, he might interview her next, and how would she explain herself to Vince?

"That was the plan," Frank answered. "Lu and I figured that if Nordhagen saw me with his daughter at her car, he might not show his face. Like I said, apparently Lu and I were right."

"And you think that is what happened?"

Frank pushed his chair back and let his elbows fall to rest upon his upper legs. He placed his forehead firmly in the heels of his hands before answering without looking up to Richter. "I don't know, Pete. I heard the shots and ran to the section of the garage where it all went down. I found Nordhagen standing next to his daughter's car...with her slumped down on the seat. I identified myself, told him to drop his weapon and get down on his knees. But I have no idea what happened in the moments that the shots were fired."

Frank looked up at Richter again. "All I can think of is that Lu may have seen Nordhagen at the car, and fearing for Miss Goodman's life...Lu fired. I don't know who fired first. Perhaps it was the jolt of being hit by a shot from Nordhagen that Lu's return shot hit Miss Goodman instead. I just don't know."

"Miss Goodman doesn't remember a thing either," said Richter as he looked back at Frank.

"Briggs is dead. So that leaves the shooter, and I'm sure he'll say anything to save his own ass."

"What are you saying?" Frank asked.

"I'm saying that it looks like we have a cop killer on the run," Richter answered. "But there are still some questions that need to be answered."

"Like what?"

Richter looked back down at his folder, flipped a few pages over until he found the one he sought. "I have a copy of your preliminary report on the Grayson case...though after Tillman finished with it, it now looks like a corrected English paper with all of his revisions and spelling changes in red. But anyway, I cross checked Briggs' cell phone records to the time you were reportedly investigating the murder scene, and I found that she made a call to Wade Donovan of all people. Did you know about that?"

"No," Frank answered, though Richter's statement confirmed how Donovan learned of Grayson's murder as quickly as he had.

"As a matter of fact, Donovan's number has appeared frequently in her phone records, both on her cell and from her home. And Briggs' phone numbers have appeared on calls he has made. I take it you don't know anything that would explain their relationship?"

"Like I said before," Frank answered. "Lu hasn't been my partner for that long. It wasn't like me and Vince, where we both knew everything about each other's lives. I knew some things about Lu, I didn't know everything."

Frank reached to the middle of the table and pushed the stop button on the tape recorder. "How long have you been investigating Briggs?"

Richter looked at Frank, then down at the still tape recorder, and then back at Frank again. "Six months."

"Why?"

Richter slowly pulled the reading glasses from his face, folded the sides and placed the frames back into his pocket. "The FBI was investigating Donovan…they tipped us off about the frequency of phone contact between him and Briggs…and more importantly, the movement of funds from him to her."

"What did the FBI have on Donovan?"

Richter shook his head. "You know the Feds. They only share enough to keep us guessing. But the little I've picked up is some theory about illegal payoffs to award city contracts with Donovan as either the deal maker or middle party."

"And you think Lula Briggs was involved?"

Richter leaned on the table, closing the distance between him and Frank. "The best thing in the eyes of the muckity-mucks at the top of the department is that we manage and clean our own house without the help of the Feds," he said quietly. "In Briggs' case, they'd rather honor a heroic officer killed in the line of duty than deal with the PR nightmare of trying to explain away another tainted cop."

Richter sat back, his fingertips on the edge of the table, his line of sight fixed upon Frank's face. "Are you okay with this, Frank?"

Frank looked away and down at the familiarity of his own hands before slowly raising his eyes across the table again. "Yeah, I'm okay with it."

Chapter Twenty-five

He had accepted the possibility that he could leave his meeting with Pete Richter as an officer suspended from the job. But to his surprise Frank was told to return to his precinct; a report would be sent to the Lieutenant in a day or two. Still, the weight of Lula's death and the stress of his performance under the grilling by Internal Affairs lingered, and as any being needing comfort Frank headed for his best friend's house.

Angie answered the sound after Frank pressed the outside button for the doorbell, her eyes reddened and swelled from washed-out tears. She should have been at work this time of day. She wasn't. She stood there in her bare feet, the unclear skin of her legs running up to the edge of faded blue shorts, the tops of which were covered by an over-sized shirt the pale color of fresh butter.

"Angie, I need to see Vince," Frank spoke in a tone void of emotion.

"He's not here," she answered, the words barely leaving her lips before she began to cry again. She turned away, leaving the door open for Frank to follow her inside.

"What's the matter, Angie?"

"Vince left me."

"What?"

"He left me. He went to his parents' house in Milwaukee."

"What happened?"

Angie wiped her sliding tears, peering at Frank above a handful of tissue. "He found your cards and letters."

"What? Oh...no, Angie," Frank pressed his palm flat against his forehead as he collapsed into a sitting position onto the couch. "I asked you to throw those away. I can't believe it. I just can't believe this. How did he find them?"

"I left them on the table. I wanted him to find them."

"You did what?" Frank asked in disbelief. "Why would you do something like *that*?"

Angie moved over to Frank, dropping to her knees, her hands holding onto his legs. "I wanted him to leave," she looked up at him through moist eyes. "It's the only way for you and I to be together. When I saw you with that young woman, I knew I couldn't let her or any other woman have you. Frank, I had to do it. It was the only way."

Frank looked around the floor at the pieces of broken plates intermingled with the ceramic body parts of a displaced figurine. A tilted mirror on the wall was marred by crooked lines reaching out from the point of impact to the edge of its frame. "I see that he didn't take it well."

"It hurt him, Frank. He was crying as much as he did when Carlo died."

"Vince has a gun stored at his parents' place, Angie. Aren't you afraid he'll kill himself?"

"He wouldn't do that," she answered. "Would he?"

Frank looked back at her, his face still locked in disbelief. "Angie, he just found out that his wife and his best friend betrayed him. What do you think?"

Frank pushed Angie aside, stood, and stepped to the fractured mirror where he was met by the eyes of his shattered reflection. "What have you done, Frank?" he asked himself softly.

"Frank," Angie's voice called from behind him, her image gliding across the cracks in the reflecting glass. "I did it for us. I did it because I love you." She cast her pleading eyes on the back of his head. "I have struggled to understand why God took my children. I have cried and cried and cried until I thought I could cry no more. And when Vince had his breakdown, I begged God to make me understand what I did to deserve the loss of everything I loved in my life. *Why* was he punishing me?" Angie's eyes turned to the reflection of Frank looking back from the mirror. "But what happened to Vince brought you and I together, Frank. It was as if after everything God took away from me, he gave me you. He gave me *us*."

The words would not come for Frank as he gazed at Angie's broken image in the glass. She reached forward, placing her small fingers on the side of his arm as her dark eyes appealed to the face in the mirror. "I have missed you so much, Frank. I need you now. I need to feel your skin pressed against mine. I need to feel your hands and your lips on my body. Please Frank, please make love to me."

Frank turned, cupping her soft shoulders firmly in his hands. "Angie, you and I will never be together again. We made a mistake. I'm sorry."

Chapter Twenty-six

Frank was awakened sharply by the rising earth beneath his freefall in a disturbing dream that ended a scant four hours of solid sleep. By the time he returned to his bed after staggering to and from the bathroom and kitchen, all he could remember of his dream was the sense of being chased and descending through the air. He tossed and turned and covered his head beneath his pillow as if doing so his ears would not hear the thoughts pursuing him into his short escapes into the sanctuary of sleep. But the voices he created were relentless and all too quickly pulled him back again to repeat the tiresome cycle until the ringing from his alarm clock finally ended the exhausting struggle.

His weariness made the time that he waited outside Donovan's office seem longer than the thirty minutes—then forty-five—then one hour as he watched every minuscule change in motion of the secretary and listened to her every word as she picked up the phone and put it down again.

"Excuse me," Frank called out to her. "You told me that Donovan was going to be busy in meetings and I haven't seen one person go into or leave his office."

"He is on conference calls, Detective," she politely answered.

"But you told him I said this was important?"

"Yes, I did."

Frank looked at his watch as another ten minutes crept past his last reading. His eyes turned to the outer entrance to the office as the door's hinges begged attention with their whine. The entering figure focused his eyes and followed their line of vision to the vacant chair next to Frank, sliding between the chrome arm rests with his left shoulder brushing up against Frank's right.

"What the hell do you think you're doing, McKay?" the Lieutenant whispered, his eyes directed to the secretary as he judged the distance that his words carried.

"I'm here to see Donovan."

"I ordered you off the Grayson case. Did I not?"

"Yeah, you did," Frank looked at him. "But this is about Lula Briggs."

The Lieutenant smiled at the secretary as she glanced over towards the two men. "I want you out of here right now. That is an order, McKay."

"How did you know I was here, Lieutenant? Did Donovan call you?"

The Lieutenant didn't answer.

"I'm going to give you a heads up, Lieutenant," Frank said softly. "I found out from Internal Affairs that the Feds are investigating Donovan. They have his phone records and are listening to all of his outgoing and incoming calls. They probably have his office bugged as well. You may want to think about the content of the conversations you have had with your pal."

The Lieutenant stared silently at Frank.

"By the gap in your open mouth, I take it that this is a bit of a surprise."

"Who told you this, McKay?"

"Pete Richter," Frank answered, reaching for his cell phone. "Give him a call if you don't believe me."

The Lieutenant gave a quick glance to the phone in Frank's hand, but shook his head rejecting the offer.

"Why do you think I'm here?" Frank continued building upon his embellishment of Pete Richter's statement. "Why do you think IA didn't suspend me? They know that the Feds are about to take Donovan down and all of those with him." Frank leaned closer to the Lieutenant and whispered. "I can understand why you don't want me to go in there and talk to him."

"You've got me all wrong on this, McKay," replied the Lieutenant. "I'm not involved in anything that Donovan is doing. We only agreed to help each other out a little."

"Like what?" Frank asked. "He helps you make Captain while you destroy evidence?"

The Lieutenant looked away from Frank, gave out a long sigh and tilted his head back against the wall with his eyes closed. He couldn't argue with the simplicity of the truth as Frank had summarized it into words. "I have wanted this promotion for a long time, McKay."

"Yeah, we all want a lot of things, Lieutenant."

The Lieutenant stood and stepped towards the secretary's desk, picking up and handing her the receiver of her phone. "Please tell your boss that

Lieutenant Tillman and Detective McKay want to see him *now*."

Donovan was a tall man, his thinness at the shoulders carrying down to his neatly pressed slacks. His light eyes flittered between Frank and the Lieutenant as he rose from his chair to meet the two police officers. "Barry, it's nice to see you again," he spoke the words slowly, flavored by the surprise that the result of his phone call to the Lieutenant had not yielded the desired result.

"Wade," the Lieutenant began in a clear, loud voice, "My detective has been waiting patiently to talk to you. I would expect that as a member of the Mayor's staff, you would understand the importance of time when an investigation is being conducted."

"Sure...ah...I apologize, Detective," Donovan replied through his confusion over the Lieutenant's comments. But in the Lieutenant's mind, if the Feds were listening in on Donovan's calls, and Frank was correct about the office being wired, this was his opportunity to offset the damage caused by his phone conversations with Donovan.

"I expect you to cooperate fully and answer all of our questions truthfully," the Lieutenant continued.

"Yes...of course, Barry."

Frank turned to the Lieutenant and pointed to his watch. "Lieutenant, don't forget you have to leave for your appointment with the Chief of Police."

"Yes," the Lieutenant replied reluctantly at Frank's ruse. "You can brief me back at the precinct later today, McKay."

Frank closed the door behind the Lieutenant as Donovan retreated to his thick, brown leather chair. "So...what questions can I answer for you, Detective? It is McKay, correct?"

"You know damn well what my name is."

"Excuse me?"

"Did you know that Lula Briggs was dead?"

"Yes," Donovan answered. "It is such a tragedy when a good police officer is killed."

"Especially one that you know well."

"Pardon me? I only met Detective Briggs once."

Frank leaned on the front of Donovan's desk, resting on the palms of his hands. "Quit the BS, Donovan. I know all about you and Briggs."

"I don't understand. You'll need to enlighten me, Detective."

The seed that Frank planted with the Lieutenant that the office could be wired by the Feds suddenly circled back in the detective's mind. What if he *was* right? He intended to confront Donovan about Lula and Jamal, but he decided that he had to be careful what he said about Lula. "Forget what I said about Briggs, Donovan," he said as he straightened out his posture. "I'm really here to ask you about Jennifer and Erin."

"Who?"

"Jennifer Goodman. You know, the girl who lived with Damon Grayson and Leo Salerno. The girl for whom you landed parts in movies being shot here in Chicago."

Donovan held up his hand. "Oh, yes. I know Jennifer. I meet so many people in my duties. I didn't know who you meant at first."

"And what about Erin? Do you remember *her*?"

Donovan fidgeted in his chair, his right leg trembling out of Frank's sight beneath his desk. "Erin...Erin...I'm not sure," he stuttered nervously.

"Really?" Frank questioned sarcastically. "Let me remind you who she was, Donovan. Erin was a 14-year old girl with blonde hair appearing in a video tape taken into evidence from Damon Grayson's apartment. It turns out that Lieutenant Tillman wasn't aware that Grayson had you on more than one tape. And you know what? Your bare white ass and your face are clearly detailed in the same tape with Erin. How *about* that!"

"What do you want, McKay?"

"I prefer to be called Detective McKay by dipwads like you, Donovan."

"What do you want?"

Frank grasped the corner of a picture frame from Donovan's desk, examining the photo of Donovan and a woman and three children. "Is this your wife and kids?"

"Yes," Donovan answered abruptly as he reached for the frame—but Frank pulled it back out of his reach.

"The coroner found out that Erin was pregnant, Donovan. My money is on you as the father."

"You can't prove that."

"I don't have to, Donovan. There are lab technicians who can prove it by matching your DNA to DNA taken from Erin's body and the fetus she was carrying." Frank looked at the picture in the frame held in his hand. "I'm standing here thinking that you're not even surprised that Erin is dead. But you probably already knew that from Salerno."

"You still haven't told me what you want," Donovan said angrily.

Frank laid the frame on the desk, picture side down. "I got what I came for, Donovan. I wanted to see you squirm...and pal, you're squirming like a fat, juicy night crawler."

Frank turned and withdrew from the office, ignoring Donovan's repeated calling of his name.

Chapter Twenty-seven

Frank pushed the up button on the outside panel of the hospital elevator. He stepped back to watch the numbers above the door light up one by one until only the number six remained bright, signaling the elevator's arrival on the 6th floor. A woman hurried past him and pressed the same button repeatedly as if her action would accelerate the machine's descent. The number five flashed and dimmed quickly before the number four illuminated and remained lit for a few seconds, prompting the Impatient Woman to return to the panel and push the up button again with rapid pokes from her finger. The 4th floor was Frank's destination—that where Jennifer Goodman remained recovering from her wound. As the Impatient Woman tapped her shoe against the tiled floor, the number four dimmed and the numbers three and two quickly flashed and muted in succession until the L on the panel above lit with the accompaniment of a dinging tone.

The door on the lobby floor split into two panels, each sliding sideways into huge gaps inside the outer wall. Frank stood to one side, keeping his hand over one half of the door as it pushed against his palm and quickly retreated back. Man and machine waited as an elderly couple shuffled out slowly, followed by a mother pushing a stroller holding a quiet, closed-eyed toddler. The Impatient Woman squeezed past the stroller and quickly pushed her finger against a button on the inside of the elevator with the speed of a Downy Woodpecker hammering into the bark of a tree. With his thoughts focused on the woman's antics Frank did not immediately register the face of the man who exited the elevator last until the silvery doors began moving towards one another.

Frank instinctively yelled out "Nordhagen!" as both of his hands intercepted the closing panels, pushing them back as he forced his body between their ends. Nordhagen turned for a moment to locate the source of the voice calling his name before he accelerated past the elderly couple and the woman with a stroller, bolting towards the front door of the hospital lobby.

Frank raced after him, yelling "Stop! Police!" The faces of the innocent people passed by both men were surprised and alarmed as they froze in their steps or quickly moved aside. Stepping into the path of the fleeing man, a security guard was quickly pushed off his feet into a row of empty chairs as Nordhagen straightened his arm against the unarmed officer's chest. Frank followed Nordhagen through the lobby entrance and across the street of humming, honking, and screeching cars—and their driver's profanities screamed at both running men. Nordhagen turned into an alley and then quickly into a narrow gangway between two garages, escaping Frank's line of sight for a fraction of a second or two. But the experienced detective chased the sound of Nordhagen's footprints and Frank again yelled "Stop! Police!" when his eyes once again fell upon the fleeing man's back.

Nordhagen burst out from the narrow canyon between two houses, knocking over a young boy whose attention had been on the music playing in his ears and the handles of a lawn mower he trailed. Frank gained a step in his chase as Nordhagen turned his head back to locate his pursuer. The burly runner darted between parked cars on both sides of a quiet street, scurrying past people who jumped out of the way as if pulling aside for a rushing emergency vehicle. The breathing deepened for both men as they continued to push their lungs and weakening legs. But Frank's legs were longer and thinner and his torso lighter than Nordhagen, whose shorter, heavier legs began to ache beneath the burden of his wide chest and slightly oversized belly. The gap between the two men shortened with each stride in their jagged race until Nordhagen swerved to his right to avoid an idle tricycle and landed on his front side atop the moist surface of a recently sprinkled lawn.

Frank fell upon the downed man from behind, pulling and pressing Nordhagen's arms down upon his back while the exhausted detective fumbled through his pockets for his handcuffs. He clicked them into place around both wrists while Nordhagen continued to resist with what little remained of his own strength. And through heavy pants of breath reaching to suck air into his tired lungs, Frank slowly recited the Miranda rights he had memorized long ago.

As his eyes followed Frank leading Nordhagen into the squad room, the Lieutenant's curiosity drew him out of his office.

"Who is this, McKay?"

"Grayson's murderer," Frank answered. "But then again, I'm off the case, right?"

The Lieutenant sneered in reply and then gazed down at Frank's soiled slacks, pointing to the green and dark stains beginning at Frank's knees. "It looks like you deserve this one, McKay. You can talk to him in Room Two. I'll watch through the glass."

Frank led Nordhagen into the interrogation room and connected the opposite end of the handcuff on the man's right wrist to the triangle brace connecting the leg to the table top. Nordhagen sat down in an armless, wood chair and pulled up with his handcuffed arm, lifting the leg of the table a half-inch or so above the floor.

"Forget it, Gunnar," Frank said while he watched him. "I've seen enough dummies who thought they could drag this table through the doorway. It's always good for a laugh, but it never works."

"Go to hell!" Nordhagen muttered.

"Watch your language, Gunnar. When you are in my house, I expect you to be civil." Frank followed his words with a quickly fading smirk. "It's okay if I call you Gunnar, right?"

"You already did, didn't you?" Nordhagen snarled with his head turned slightly away.

Frank circled slowly around the table. "Your voice carries a lot of hostility, Gunnar."

"So what, cop!"

Frank leaned over the table. "Hey, you can call me Detective, or McKay, or Detective McKay, but don't call me cop." Nordhagen kept his defiant eyes pointed at Frank, and the experienced officer backed off slowly to give the man's rebelliousness room to breathe.

"I take it that you don't like policemen?"

"No," Nordhagen replied as his eyes followed Frank. "I hate *cops*, prison guards, shysters, and judges...all of you."

Frank remembered what he had learned from Sal Martin—that part of Nordhagen's prison time was for assaulting a police officer. "Is that why you sent a police officer to the hospital?"

"The other one should have gone, too. I guess I didn't hit *him* hard enough."

"They were just doing their jobs, Gunnar. You had no reason to beat them. What, you couldn't get your fill of violence by beating up on your wife and kids?"

"You don't know nothing about me!" Nordhagen argued back. "And for those two cops...it was just a matter of getting even."

"Why? What did they do to you?"

"Nothing," Nordhagen muttered as looked away.

"It had to be something, Gunnar. What were you getting even for?"

Nordhagen glared back at Frank, his stained teeth displayed in the bitterness of his memories. "Because...when I was a kid and my old lady called the cops because my father was drunk...they'd show up, drag him off to jail and beat the snot out of him. He was a small guy like me and they were big cops. But it made them feel bigger when they could gang up on him...in *their house*." Nordhagen's last two words were pushed towards Frank with unflinching resentment.

Frank stood straight, placing his hands on his hips. He lowered the tone in his voice. "No one is going to touch you in here, Gunnar." Frank was careful not to use the word 'house' again, having seen the rage disturbed in Nordhagen at the push of that button.

"Gunnar, I'm going to ask you again. Do you want a lawyer?"

Nordhagen shook his head that he didn't.

"What were you doing at the hospital?"

"Trying to see my daughter...but there was a cop in the hallway outside her room."

"Did you want to hurt her?"

"No!"

"Then why were you there?"

"I wanted to see her...to make things right between us."

Frank read the change in Nordhagen's expression as the energy in the man's face that had worked so hard to display anger, relaxed into a glimpse of the man's truth. Nordhagen looked away and then back to Frank as the detective sat down in the chair on the opposite side of the table.

"When I was in prison," he began in words lower and careful in tone, "My worthless lawyer was the only visitor I ever had. My wife, my two sons, my Berta...none of *them* ever came to see me...none of them ever bothered to write."

"It must have been tough," uttered Frank as he began to sense the man's pain.

Nordhagen looked at him and nodded. "It was...especially when the other guys had wives or kids or girlfriends coming to see them all the time. It made me think about things..."

"Like what?" Frank asked as Nordhagen's word's faded into silence. "Like maybe you drove them all away because you were just like *your* father?"

"Yes," Nordhagen whispered as he avoided Frank's eyes.

"And that's why you violated your parole and came looking for your daughter?"

"Yes."

"How did you find her?"

Nordhagen's cheeks puffed as he held and released a mouth full of air. "After I got released I went back to where I had lived...you know, looking for my family. They were all gone. My old landlady didn't have any idea where my wife took my two sons, but she gave me a box of old mail. And in there were letters addressed to my wife with the return address from Chicago from someone named Jennifer Goodman."

"And that's how you found your daughter?"

Nordhagen nodded. "I read the letters. They were from Berta to her mother. She told my wife that she was living in Chicago with an older man, but she also asked for forgiveness because of the things he made her do."

"What kind of things?"

"I don't know. Berta just wrote that they made her feel ashamed...and she blamed it on me, her father."

"Do you still have these letters?"

"They're back at my room," Nordhagen answered. "If the cockroaches haven't carried them off."

"What happened at Grayson's apartment?" Frank asked, feeling ready he had reached the point in the conversation between the two men that he could ask that question. "We have your fingerprints from his apartment and on the gun you dropped in the parking garage. And we matched the bullets taken from Grayson's body to your gun, Gunnar."

"What about that guy I shot in the garage? What happened to him?"

"That's not my case, Gunnar," Frank replied. "I only care about what happened to Grayson. That's why I was at the garage, Gunnar. I was interviewing your daughter about Grayson."

The door opened behind Frank. "McKay, I need to see you *now*," the Lieutenant ordered.

"I'll be back, Gunnar," Frank said as he followed the Lieutenant, closing the door behind him.

"What kind of crap are you pulling, McKay?" grilled the Lieutenant in a subdued voice. "I want you to get him to admit to shooting Briggs, not just Grayson"

"Briggs isn't my case, Lieutenant," Frank contested. "You told me that and Richter told me that."

"I don't care. We have him in here. Let's get him for both murders."

"I don't want to step on Richter's shoes on this one, Lieutenant."

"Just do what you're told to do, McKay."

Frank threw open his arms. "If you want me to blow your case for the sake of Richter's...then fine, that's your call. But I'll tell you *this*. I've got Nordhagen ready to lock into a confession for killing Grayson, but the moment I tell him that he killed Briggs and that she was a cop, he'll lawyer up and not say another word to me. If he confesses to killing

Grayson, the fact that you destroyed evidence has less chance of being an issue. And if he confesses to killing Grayson before he faces a charge of killing a cop, he's more likely to cave in to shooting Lu also. You do it my way, your ass is covered. But if you want it done your way, then fine."

Frank turned abruptly for the door.

"McKay!" the Lieutenant called after him. "Do it your way."

Frank returned to his chair across from Nordhagen. "Sorry, Gunnar," he began convincingly. "My dipwad of a boss thinks I'm being too soft on you. So why did you want to see your daughter again?"

Nordhagen looked directly into Frank's eyes, pausing for a moment as he felt relief that he found another human willing to listen to his unshared burden, that he *had* killed Grayson. "I wanted to ask Berta to forgive me and tell me where her mother and brothers were. Grayson said she didn't live there any longer. I asked him if he had any pictures of her. He showed me one. And then he said he also had her on video tape and would be willing to sell me a copy for a grand."

"Did he tell you what was on the tapes?"

"He didn't have to," Nordhagen answered. "His face said it all. So I got mad and started going through his video tapes, throwing things around...and he told me to get out. He threatened to call the police. Then I turned to look at him and he had this smug look on his face. And just as I was going to leave, he told me that my daughter was good in bed. So I shot the bastard."

"And you took his address book?"

"Yes, that's how I found Berta. Grayson had written an address in his book for Jennifer Goodman...

but when I found that building, the apartment was listed for some guy named Salerno. I watched the building everyday for hours before I saw her. And then I followed her to that park by the lake where I saw her with you."

"I have two daughters who are around Berta's age," Frank interrupted to keep Nordhagen from talking about the shooting in the garage. But in admitting he was also a father, Frank continued his strategy to earn Nordhagen's trust—at least long enough to win over the man's signature at the bottom of a confession statement.

Chapter Twenty-eight

"I didn't think I'd see you again," the priest said as he stood with Frank in the quiet of the church.

"I didn't either, Dave. But I'm here now."

"Do you want me to hear your confession?"

"No."

The priest nodded. "I sensed the other day that you had a voice inside that screamed to be heard."

"Don't do this, Dave. Don't try to save me."

"Then why did you come here, Frank?"

"I need a favor from an old friend. I need you to put aside that collar for a little while," Frank answered in a soft voice amplified in the surrounding emptiness.

"Okay...what can I do?"

"I need advice. If you had sensitive material that could destroy the Mayor's run to be Governor, which television station would you go to?"

The two men talked for nearly two hours before Frank left, the priest holding an oversized, sealed envelope that Frank had carried in with him.

The flowers that Frank carried through the 4th floor corridor on his way to Jennifer Goodman's room were a colorful contrast to the handgun tucked in the holster beneath his jacket. Under his other arm, he carried a cardboard box pressed between the inside of his upper arm and the side of his chest. He found Jennifer sitting up in bed, her left arm held across her chest in a white sling. Leo Salerno stood at her bedside, his magnified eyes inspecting Frank and the bouquet of yellows, whites, pinks, and lavenders bunched together in green wrapping.

"Leo, why don't you take a walk," Frank suggested after an initial exchange of greetings. Frank waited until Salerno vanished around the corner of the doorway before he handed the bright bundle to Jennifer.

"Did I get you into trouble?" Jennifer asked with a faint smile across her lightly glossed lips.

"You mean by what you told Pete Richter?"

"Yes...that we were on a date."

Frank shook his head. "No. But I'll give you credit for a nice try at it."

"I heard that you arrested my father yesterday. Is that true?"

"Yeah," Frank answered. "He confessed to Grayson's murder."

"Will he go back to prison?"

"For a long time."

"Good, he deserves to be locked away."

Frank studied her face, wondering if those words were spoken from the outside of her heart. "After talking with your father, I don't know if I should call you Jennifer or Berta. I can't say one name without thinking the other."

"I'm Jennifer now," she answered, curling her lip on one side of her mouth. "I don't ever want to be Berta again."

"There's no excuse for what your father did...to you, your mother, for killing Grayson. But you need to know that he came to Chicago to find you because he wanted your forgiveness."

"I don't care."

"Well, you should...for you own good. Regardless of what he did before, he saved your life in that garage, Jennifer. In that moment he was your father and you were his daughter."

"Why are you telling me these things?"

Frank looked into her eyes as she stubbornly held back her tears. "I guess because I'm a father, too."

"What's in the box?" Jennifer pointed with her free hand.

Frank placed the carton down upon the white linen surface of her bed, lifting the upper cardboard folds slowly as he began to answer her question. "I stunk up the oven in my kitchen pretty bad last night while I did this," he said before pulling out a huge jagged rectangle of black plastic. "This is all that remains of Grayson's video tapes of you."

"Why?" she asked as her free hand touched the top surface of the black clump.

"Everyone deserves a break. But this isn't just about you, Jennifer. The men who were on these tapes were being blackmailed. And for those men who had wives and family, they paid as big a price as you did."

"Thank you, Detective McKay," Jennifer offered, her hand held outward to his.

"You're welcome, but what you do from now on out is up to you. You've got to make the right choices, and giving up your body because you think that's the only way...well, you need to believe and respect yourself. Jeez, listen to me. I *am* talking like a father."

Jennifer responded with a little laugh beneath her tears.

"And the first thing you need to do for yourself when you get out of the hospital," Frank continued, "is to get away from Leo. Find someone your own age. Make the effort to find your mother and brothers. But don't go back to living with that dipwad."

Jennifer smiled.

As he walked towards the elevator, Frank thought about the things he had said to Jennifer. He wondered if he had made a fool of himself. He wondered if he had come off as sounding too preachy. He shrugged his shoulders. He said what he said and it was too late to take it all back.

"Detective!" Salerno's voice called from down the hall. He hurried his steps, catching up to Frank at the elevator door. "Jennifer's doctor is releasing her tomorrow...so I'll be taking her home."

"That's good," Frank said unconvincingly.

"Yes, it is. I was wondering if you have given any more thought to my offer."

"You mean about the tapes?"

"Yes."

The door opened, Frank stepped into the elevator and turned to face Salerno. "Yeah, I left the tapes in Jennifer's room, Leo."

Chapter Twenty-nine

The second thoughts loitered patiently for the buzz of the alarm clock, pouncing on Frank's mind the moment the circled stream of water washed away his bridge to dreams forgotten. His doubts nagged him through his mundane morning ritual of stroking the hairs off his face. And as he stared back at the eyes looking back at his from inside the silver-backed glass, he listened to the scolding voice admonish him for his foolish decision.

"You idiot! You stupid idiot!" echoed the voice in the mirror. "You threw away all that money for someone who will never think of you again...for someone who will likely go back to doing what she always did. You idiot!"

Frank increased the volume on his car radio, hoping the deep bass in the music would shake off the haunting grumble of second opinion. But the little voices were too loud, too many, and they were pushed back only long enough to regain their strength and rush back at him once again.

"I am such an idiot!" he said aloud over the beat of the song pulsating from the speakers. He pounded the heel of his hand on the steering wheel as he wondered if there was anything in his life that he could do that would be right—just once. Even when he thought he was making the correct choice, it seemed so wrong now that he replayed his actions back again. He still didn't have the money to contribute to Molly's wedding. He betrayed and hurt his best friend. And through the fog of his feelings for Angie, he wasn't sure the emotion and passion were worth the nagging guilt he felt in what he may have done to the Corelli's marriage.

Guilt. He pondered why he had the presence of blame over Vince and Angie and the absence of any responsibility for Lula's death. "That wasn't my fault," he answered his thoughts, which in return questioned if Lula would have shot around him had he stood where Nordhagen stood. He wondered how he would have felt if it was his gun that felled Lula trying to protect Jennifer. No—what happened to Briggs was not his doing.

"Why couldn't I have been like her?" he asked himself silently as he pondered how Lula could allow herself to take money from Donovan. Frank was on the edge with Salerno's offer. He could taste the crossing of that line, but he was missing something or had too much of something else. Was it courage, or fear, or foolhardiness, or some other unknown he had yet to recognize?

Once at the precinct house, Frank found an excuse to escape the hold of his morning thoughts by focusing on the paperwork needed to submit his beneficiary revision on his life insurance policy. He was removing Mickey's name and replacing his brother with an uneven split between his daughters, Molly and Megan McKay. But Molly's name would be changing in December, and Frank could not remember her fiancé's last name. He hated any paperwork between him and Insurance companies and he had no desire to submit a change request now—only to do it again at the end of the year. He called Molly's cell number, and when she didn't answer, he left a message. "This is your Dad. Can you call me back or leave me a message. I need to know Blake's last name. You know...your future last name. Bye." He could wait one more day.

Frank's head lifted upward as he sensed a figure approaching his desk.

"Lieutenant," Frank acknowledged the man as he folded the papers and placed them in his top drawer.

"Thanks for asking McKay, I'm doing just fine today. I'm just waiting for the other shoe to fall," the Lieutenant responded with the same tone of sarcasm he was hardened to hearing from Frank. "In the meantime, Chicago isn't about to let us just sit around. You need to get over to this address. It was called in as a double homicide."

"Who should I take with me?" Frank asked, looking around the squad room.

"You're on your own on this one, McKay."

Frank arrived at the scene just ahead of the car carrying the three recognizable faces from the SOCO team. Ted Schwack pulled his tall frame out of the back seat, his camera dangling around his long neck. John Coomer closed the front seat passenger door behind him and moved directly to the popped-up open trunk, grabbing the large black bag that carried his brushes and powder and plastic bags and vials. And Sal Martin waved towards Frank as he stepped from the driver's seat, locking the car doors with a point of his hand as he walked away with a clip board tucked under his arm beneath a short-sleeved white shirt.

The uniformed officers outside the small bungalow briefed Frank and Sal on the identities of the married couple inside while John and Ted passed them all, entering the strangers' home to begin their evidence gathering.

As Ted stood over the bodies, the flashes of his camera capturing what was already still, Frank and Sal carefully walked through and examined the details of the scene. The woman's head was at rest against the uppermost corner of a plastic covered couch. If not for the blood on her silky white slip and the lack of motion in her chest, she looked as though she had fallen asleep while watching television—though no set was in the room. Her feet were snuggled in pink fuzzy slippers. Her one hand, resting at her side, loosely held the panty hose that never made it onto her legs. Both the deep scarlet color on her lips and the soft glow upon her pale skin appeared to be freshly applied. In the couple's bathroom, where damp towels hung over an open shower door and on the tiled floor, an open makeup bag sat on an aged vanity illuminated by lights alive with energy above a mirror on the wall. At the foot of an unmade bed in another room were the misty rose dress that was to be pulled over her slip, and the shoes that were to replace the pink slippers on her feet. Surely by now her coworkers must have wondered if she was caught up in the morning's traffic.

With the tips of his latex gloves, Frank turned the letter lying open on the top of a bedroom dresser, reading the type printed words beneath the letterhead of the mortgage company. He wondered if the key to what happened in this house were the words '3rd Notice' on the subject line, or the word 'foreclosure'—or a combination of both.

Back in the room of the murder, the body of the woman's husband was sprawled on the floor, a gun still held, if lazily, in his hand—his head lying in the red stain spread unevenly into the worn out blue carpet.

Sal stepped to Frank's side. "Well, Frank," he said in a matter of fact tone. "The proof will be in the ballistics report, but this one looks like a murder-suicide to me."

"Yeah," Frank responded. "While we're waiting for Bali to get here, I'll see what the neighbors have to say. If you find an address book or something, I'll contact their relatives."

Frank spent the balance of his shift talking to strangers, asking questions, and trying to deflect the questions of curiosity posed to him in return. He knocked on doors that did not open, he stood on doorsteps when doors opened guardedly, and he sat uncomfortably in stranger's homes. He left messages on phones answered by machines and talked to voices for which there was no matching face. And when he returned to the precinct house, he summarized in black ink on white paper what he believed happened as the deceased couple began their final morning.

It felt good to his mind when his long shift came to an end and he returned to his apartment again. He felt better when he opened the lone item in his mailbox. It was an envelope with Molly's name and address on the little sticker in the left-hand corner. Inside the envelope was a greeting card with an illustration in pastel colors of an adult man and little girl. The girl's head was pointed upward towards the man, whose eyes were fixed downward in return over a smile as wide as the face upon which it was drawn. The little girl's arm reached upward, her hand wrapped around the man's larger hand. The print below the illustration read "No Matter What...". Frank opened the card and inside was a loose photograph of Molly with Blake covering the conclusion of the front of the card. "...You will always be my Dad."

And below the line where she had written *'Love, Molly'* was another line in her handwriting in which she had written, *'PS. Trust me, Dad. Megan will come around.'*

Frank leaned the photograph against a book on a shelf in his small living room and walked into the kitchen with his lips curved in a warm smile. He pulled a TV Dinner from his uncluttered freezer, placed it in his heated oven, set the timer and turned on the small television on his kitchen counter in time for the local newscast.

If the tease before the commercials was true, Father Dave delivered with his favor. Frank waited anxiously for the newscast and the scandal to begin, and he was not disappointed as the words read by the neatly dressed anchorman were the first indication that Wade Donovan's world was about to crash and crash hard.

The oven timer had almost completed the descent to zero when the news anchors closed their afternoon show. The "buzz...buzz...buzz" from the other room indicated that someone wanted to get through the security entrance on the bottom floor of the apartment building. Frank rushed to his front door, pressed the intercom button and asked, "Who is it?" But as he did and before he heard a reply, the oven timer in the kitchen signaled it had reached its goal. Frank pressed another button to allow access to the person buzzing below before he rushed back into the kitchen, where he grabbed a dish towel and used it to remove his dinner from the oven.

Just as he slid the dinner plate onto his small, bare table, a swift thump-thump-thump from the outside surface of the front door echoed through his apartment. Frank shouted. "Just come in...the door's unlocked!"

After the door opened with a low-pitched creak and closed with a muffled thud, Frank returned to the living room to face the familiar figure that had entered. Their eyes met one another's in silence before Frank looked downward at the dark circle in the barrel of the handgun aimed towards him. His eyes rose again. "You don't have to do this," he said softly.

His words had barely escaped their wake before Frank reeled backward from the force that slammed into his right shoulder—his left hand following instinctively as his right knee collapsed to the floor. He pulled his bloodied hand away. The lines of his palm were covered by a miniature sea of dark red. He raised his eyes again, looking past the pointed gun and into the eyes now glaring down at him.

"I'm sorry," Frank forced the words through his pain just before a second sharp poke slammed into his chest, crumpling his legs beneath him. His back hit the floor with a jolt forcing his lungs to gasp for air. His vision rolled across the white ceiling as his tongue sensed the taste and the feel of his blood rising through the inside of his mouth. As the ringing in his ears subsided he picked up the softer sounds again. His breathing shortened to rapid little humps. The shooter's footsteps moved away until the door opened again with a slow creak and closed with a gentle thud.

Frank listed his head to the side. His eyes searched frantically until they found the photograph of Molly; and he held her in his stare until the yellowish light screamed in his ears and pulled him into total darkness.

Gary Pisarski

Gary Pisarski is a lifelong resident of Chicago and Northern Illinois, where he currently resides with his wife and children. Having had several poems and magazine articles published years ago, he rekindled his story telling energy in his first book, BLACK RIVER CROSSING, an historical novel. AFTER THE DOOR OPENED is Mr. Pisarski's second novel.

Both of these titles are available at
www.garypisarski.npauthors.com and
at www.nightengalepress.com,
on all online bookstores, and upon request in
your favorite bricks and mortar bookstore.

Printed in the United States
73685LV00002B/155

9 781933 449388